BIG NOISE

Big Noise © 2009 by Jennifer Lynn Wright
All rights reserved.

Clover Valley Press, LLC
6286 Homestead Rd.
Duluth, MN 55804-9621
USA

This is a work of fiction. Any resemblance between characters in this book and actual persons, living or dead, is coincidental.

Cover design by Sally Rauschenfels
Cover images © iStockPhoto.com:
    Julia Freeman-Woolpert (figure in snowy field)
    Royce DeGrie (gun)

Author photo by Helen Mongan-Rallis

Printed in the United States of America on acid-free paper

Library of Congress Control Number: 2009925881

ISBN-13: 978-0-9794883-4-4
ISBN-10: 0-9794883-4-6

BIG NOISE

A Jo Spence Mystery

JEN WRIGHT

CLOVER VALLEY PRESS, LLC
DULUTH, MINNESOTA

Acknowledgments

No book reaches print without the help of many fantastic people. My books are probably needier than most. The following people contributed to *Big Noise,* and I owe them thanks and whatever else they want.

A special acknowledgment must go to Cathy Coon, who provided all of the poetry in the book with the exception of the final poem. Thank you so much.

Lynn Boggie provided me with information about volunteer fire departments. Diane Dickey suggested the "love is like a heartbeat" scene. You both helped me to better understand rural Minnesota. I am indebted to Fran Kaliher for living a life that inspired the home and character of Amanda. Scott and Tommy Hanna provided background information about rural volunteer fire fighting and information on handguns.

Judith Torrence, Mary Anne Daniel, Karen Andrews, and Gail Polesak supported me in numerous ways along the journey. Karen Andrews and Jane Hovland provided feedback about the character Donald and the realism of his mental health issues. Lynn Walker provided information about methamphetamine addiction and overdose symptoms.

Sue Lawson and Ellen O'Neill gave me valuable commentary on the early manuscript. Char Appelwick and Jim Madden generously read the final manuscript prior to printing. I am grateful to Joyce Snyder for acting as a beta reader. Lori L. Lake's Minneapolis writers group was also generous with feedback and advice. My writers group, including Char Appelwick, Charlene Brown, Dianna Hunter, and Nancy Gallagher, helped me to work my way through the entire project. Thank you for your encouragement and wisdom.

Thanks go to all of the dogs in my life for giving me lots to write about. Lastly, thank you, Kari, for your unwavering support. I know that between my bouts of binge reading and writing, I neglected you. Your support means the world to me. You mean the world to me.

For Charlene Brown
my friend, mentor, editor, and publisher

Thank you so much for your gentle guidance. I was so vulnerable and insecure when I started writing, and you helped me to discover a part of myself that brings me so much inner joy. I would not have done any of this without you.

Prologue

Trouble has a way of finding me. That's what my friends always say. Zoey and I had every intention of taking time to relax and enjoy our two-week vacation in the snowy north woods. Our destination, a cozy rural outpost called Big Noise, should have been ideal for a romantic getaway. Our friends were welcoming, and we loved the neighborly spirit of the community. Yet, even here I stumbled into a situation that could prove deadly. Once again, I placed myself and Zoey in harm's way.

I was thinking about that as I tried desperately to second-guess a madman and to calculate my chances of survival. This time, trouble hadn't come looking for me. I had gone looking for him.

One thick door separated me from Zoey. I could feel Don's eyes watching me think about that door. He took the butt of the gun and hit the hard, unyielding wood, yelling, "Shut up, or I'll kill her."

Chapter 1

Jo and Zoey settled onto the floor of their rented cabin for a cup of French-pressed dark roast. The woodstove was doing a slow burn on two birch logs that their hosts Sandy and Ree had cut and split by hand. Jo's two dogs were snoring softly in front of the fire.

As Jo savored her coffee, Zoey set her cup down on the hearth and settled into Jo's strong arms, murmuring, "This is so nice."

Jo held her lover and leaned back against the front of a well-worn couch, which had been transformed by the simple addition of a handmade quilt. Jo smiled inwardly as she touched the tan and green squares sewn into longer pieces of corduroy. She knew some woman had lovingly stitched each piece, not really thinking about her work as art. Jo admired the patience it took to build this quilt. She would never have been able to sit still long enough to sew one, let alone create something this intricate.

She and Zoey barely had time to be together, it seemed to her, let alone to indulge in artistic pursuits. Though they had been lovers for only a few months, their respective jobs had interfered with both the quality and the quantity of time that they had to spend with each other. Jo's position as Juvenile Probation Supervisor in Duluth, Minnesota, and Zoey's tenure-track professorship at the university were both demanding of their time and energy.

Zoey had suggested on the ride up that it would be nice for them to reconnect and talk after another hectic week. Jo, on the other hand, had found herself wanting to spend the entire two weeks of their planned vacation in bed.

Her intense work life, dealing with juveniles who had run afoul of the law and needed persistent guidance and monitoring, kept her days busy and her talents engaged. She often worried about the welfare of her staff as well. Sometimes she felt like a nurse in an intensive care unit. Taking a break might cost someone's life.

When she was off duty, her time with Zoey was equally if not more intense. Even when they told each other that tonight they should really get some sleep, they ended up having sex well into the early morning hours. At age forty, Jo was starting to feel the strain, but she couldn't help herself. The sex was likely to taper off as time went on, but Jo hoped that wouldn't be anytime soon.

She was more in love with Zoey after just a few short months than she had ever been with anyone before. Maybe the life-and-death experience they had shared as their relationship was forming had something to do with it.

Jo flashed on the night at her home when she and Zoey had knocked out a crazed killer in her shop. She remembered the almost total darkness. Without a rehearsal and no second chance to get it right, Zoey had flipped on the light switch at the exact instant when Jo had swung the crowbar to take down the hit man. Jo wondered if Zoey kept replaying that scene over and over in her mind, too.

She knew they both needed this vacation, but letting go of work and totally relaxing might be a stretch for Jo. Her thoughts often focused on crime and the temptations that juveniles were prey to. She couldn't go into a store without eyeing the place for shoplifters, or leave items in plain sight in her car, fearing would-be thieves. She even found herself ranting to her friends about the lack of security in their homes.

What kind of crime could they have way out here in Big Noise? she asked herself. *Plenty,* came her unbidden but candid reply. Then she caught herself. Working in the criminal justice system gave one a true view of the amount of bad behavior going on, but it didn't help to become so jaded that you overlooked the good in people.

Big Noise, a community located forty miles north of Jo's home in Duluth and twenty miles inland from Lake Superior, was composed of several hundred scattered residences. It was settled during the logging boom of the early 1900s. The loggers would come out of the woods after a hard day of work, drawn to a tavern by the noise. A village developed near this social meeting place, and the name Big Noise just stuck.

Jo enjoyed coming here to visit her good friends Sandy and Ree and to experience the close-knit community that these two women were so much a part of—Sandy as the town's postmistress and Ree as a physician who volunteered on the ambulance crew for area emergencies. They had their responsibilities and stresses, but the pace seemed easier here than in Duluth.

Looking down at Zoey, whose eyes were half closed, Jo's thoughts returned to the present and to the luxury of having Zoey in her arms for hours and days and endless nights. When they made love, Jo's mind let go of everything, and she was open in a way that she had never thought possible with a lover. She hoped that this deep-woods retreat would be just what she needed to get away from it all and give Zoey her undivided attention.

Zoey's eyes were fully open now, and she was looking at Jo with curiosity.

"What are you thinking about so hard?"

"I'm hoping that the bed is comfortable," Jo gave Zoey her most winsome smile.

"You have a one-track mind, which is one of the things I like best about you."

Zoey snuggled in closer, and Jo breathed in the smell of her short dark hair. "You don't wish I was more complicated, so you could use that brilliant psychoanalytic brain of yours to figure me out?"

"Nope, I've already figured you out. You're a bit compulsive, but I think you have a pure heart. Besides, the university provides me with plenty of undergraduates if I want to indulge in mental health diagnostics."

Jo knew that Zoey and her friend Donna were surveying every student who used the university's health center, testing for psychological problems, regardless of what ailment prompted their visit.

"How's that going?"

Zoey's whole face brightened as she described her research.

"It's going great!" She flashed a gorgeous smile. "Donna and I have been getting tons of data."

"So, what are you finding? Anything exciting?"

"We've found a lot of students with anxiety, some with depression, and we've even uncovered a few serious disorders that might have gone undetected if we hadn't been screening."

As Jo listened, she wondered how anyone could find data-crunching so fascinating, but she loved how smart and secure with herself Zoey seemed when she talked about her studies.

"What serious disorders did you find?" Jo raised her eyebrows.

"Well, we found two students who'd been hearing voices but never told anyone."

"What did you do?"

"We referred them to the community mental health center. They'll get meds and therapy."

"That's good."

"One really interesting case popped up last week. The guy didn't admit this to me, or even realize it was happening, but I believe I can accurately diagnose him with dissociative identity disorder."

Jo wasn't following.

"It used to be called multiple personality disorder. Or MPD."

"Is it dangerous?"

"It can be. It depends on the types of personalities present and what role they have in the overall functioning of the person. Usually one personality is the protector. I think I saw him briefly as I witnessed changes in the client's demeanor."

"Wow! You weren't alone with him, were you?"

"No. Because of the study's protocols, I had Donna with me."

"Geez, are you still seeing him?"

"No. He wouldn't accept a referral, either. He may come back for help at some point. Donna will call me if that happens."

Jo didn't relish the thought of this guy being anywhere near Zoey, but she wanted to trust that her partner knew what she was doing in her work life.

"What else are you finding?"

"Well, primarily we see depression. Some PTSD. Some problems combined with addiction."

Jo tried her best to stay focused on the study, but being in such close proximity with Professor Rundell was proving too much for her.

Suddenly, she wrestled Zoey down to the ground and said, "You know what that academic stuff does to me. You've gone too far this time!"

Feigning resistance, Zoey said, "What are you going to do about it?"

Jo decided to let her actions speak for themselves, and she began to undo Zoey's purple flannel shirt one button at a time. Again Zoey feigned resistance. In order to relieve Zoey of her shirtsleeves, Jo had to move her knees, which were immobilizing Zoey's arms. This gave Zoey an opportunity to turn the tables on her. She bucked her back up, flipped Jo over, and then pinned her down.

"OK, tough girl, what are you gonna do now?" she intoned.

She slowly unzipped Jo's fleece until she had it completely open.

Just when it looked like she was in the same predicament Jo had been in, not knowing how she could undress her without releasing Jo's arms, she simply pulled her bra up, exposing her breasts. Zoey lowered herself so that their chests were nearly touching, stopped, then sat upright, put her arms up in the air, and flexed her biceps.

"I am so in control here."

As quickly as the playfulness had begun, it turned into something more serious. Jo looked into Zoey's green, almost emerald eyes and thought, *Whatever happens, I hope I don't screw this up or let her down.*

"Let's go up to the loft," Zoey whispered.

"OK," Jo agreed. But before following Zoey up the narrow ladder, she reached for the exquisite quilt and carried it up to the bed they would share this night.

Chapter 2

A WHILE LATER, UNABLE TO SLEEP, Jo got quietly up, trying not to disturb Zoey, and came back down the ladder. She stoked the fire with an all-night log, closed the damper, and gave her two dogs a rub. Java, a black lab with a white spot on his chest, and Cocoa, a springer chocolate lab mix, had been a little out of sorts because they couldn't climb up the ladder to get to the bed. They had whimpered for a while and finally settled into the couch below. The soft red glow of the fire flickered and played off the logs of the cabin's side walls.

Jo sometimes worried that her job would begin to wear on Zoey. Getting calls at all hours of the night, working late, and being hauled knee-deep into serious criminal matters had become almost routine for her. She was hoping that Zoey, even if she didn't exactly like these intrusions on their life together, could at least develop a tolerance for her line of work. This, more than anything, would give them a fighting chance.

But Jo knew that she often put herself in harm's way. Hell, she'd placed both of them in harm's way. So far, Zoey had been supportive rather than angry.

Jo shrugged into her parka and slipped out the cabin door. The moon was rising above the treeline, and Jo looked into its distant face.

What have I done in my life to deserve this happiness? And how long will it last?

Before she could fathom an answer, she felt a vibration coming from her coat pocket.

Cell towers must be going up everywhere, she thought to herself as she groped for her phone.

"Jo Spence, Juvenile Probation."

"Jo, it's me, Nate." Sergeant Jerome Nathan was Jo's primary contact in the Duluth Police Department. "Sorry to bother you so late, and I know you're supposed to be on vacation, but I just talked with a homeless teen who gave me some news. I thought you'd want to hear it right away."

"What's happened?"

"We picked up a runaway tonight who says she's been hanging out with Rick Thomas—you know, the kid you had as a juvie? Get this…she says he disappeared three weeks ago when they went up to Big Noise to stash some stolen property."

The phone cut out suddenly, and Jo hit redial.

"Nate, are you there…?"

The call went through right away, and Nate said, "Yeah."

"OK, so Rick is in trouble again?"

"Sounds like it. You know, he never stopped being an addict, no matter how hard you tried to help him."

"He could be a really sweet kid when he wasn't high. He was one I always worried about, though—he couldn't handle life on the streets without some kind of escape." Jo thought about his messed up family—a dad who beat the shit out of him and a drug-addicted mother. Jo had tried to help him get his life together. During the last eight years, she'd stayed in touch, off and on, trying to keep him on track.

She didn't often adopt her clients like that after their probationary stints expired, but with Rick it was different. After investing countless evenings in him, she couldn't just let go and hope for the best. Plus, after a while, she found that she really liked him. With a junkie, that was risky. But she had her reasons for hanging in there with him.

She couldn't forget the time when she had been cornered in an alley by a group of teenaged boys intent on showing her what manly men they were. He had stepped into the alley opening, a silhouette of pure determination.

"Get lost, or I'm taking every one of you out. I mean it!"

The punks had scattered in every direction. Jo could take care of herself in almost any situation, but that night she had wondered if her luck had run out. No matter how many times she rescued Rick, it wouldn't make her feel any less grateful to him for that moment of personal loyalty and courage.

"His girlfriend said he went into the woods and never came out again. She was too strung out and paranoid to report it, though, so he's either in trouble or long gone by now."

"Shit! Where exactly was he last seen?" Her phone went dead again. This time, Nate was the first to get a signal through.

"Listen, Jo. Missing persons isn't really your thing. Maybe I should have waited to tell you when you got back to work."

"No, Nate—this is personal. In spite of his troubles, we really connected. I feel like I owe it to him to try to track him down and see if he needs some help. What's the girlfriend's name and number?"

"Katie Shantree. She's supposed to have family up there. When we picked her up, she was terrified that we were going to transport her back home. Something isn't right there. I'm holding her in detention for the time being, so there's no direct phone number I can give you. Maybe when you get back in town, you could talk to her." Nate hesitated a little too long.

"If you ask around about the Shantrees up there, you'll track the family down. They're infamous in Big Noise. You know the type. Junk cars all over the yard. Half of 'em on probation at any given time. Be careful there, Jo."

Jo nodded into the phone as if he could see her.

"Did you hear me? I said be careful. Her older brothers are likely dealers. For sure, they're criminals of opportunity."

"Oh, don't worry, Nate. I'll keep it low-key."

"Do you know what Rick was into recently?"

"Well, the last time I talked to him, he had a job as a mason."

Nate didn't think he still had that job, not according to his information from the runaway. "Maybe he got into using meth and made the jump to cooking it. If not, maybe he had a bad stretch of using and had enough sense to quit his job before getting fired."

"He's a good guy. I mean, he's a follower, you know? I can't see him getting involved in selling." Jo knew her bias was showing.

"He's stayed in touch with you, hasn't he?"

"Every few months. He calls when he's doing well, or when he's really in trouble. I haven't heard from him in quite a while, though. Maybe six months."

"You can't save 'em all, Jo."

"Just this one?"

"OK, I'll give you this one. How about I talk to our Drug Task Force guys, see if we can find out who his dealer was?"

"Thanks, Nate, I'll owe you one."

"Wait to see what I turn up, then make it a double."

"I'm glad you called. I'll nose around a bit, since I'm up here anyway. Don't worry."

The phone lost its signal again before Nate could dissuade her.

Chapter 3

WHEN THE MORNING LIGHT came creeping into their loft, Jo opened her eyes to see Zoey looking at her with awe and appreciation.

"What?"

"I need to look at you. You're so beautiful."

Jo managed an embarrassed "Huh?" She had never really thought much about what she looked like. She had always approached her looks with a utilitarian view. She knew she was tall, and strong. She was lean from all of the outdoor activities she enjoyed, and from her healthy love for sports of all kinds, but she never really thought about her looks at all. She'd been told by many people that her short, dark, unruly curls were a gift, and that she had beautiful blue eyes, but she chocked it up to being lucky.

Now, for the first time in her life, Jo felt truly desired. She basked in the hungry, possessive look in her lover's eyes.

Jo took Zoey by the hand and guided her down the ladder and into the main cabin. After building a fire from the previous night's coals, she placed a thick towel in front of the stove. After she had a roaring fire going, she filled a bowl with water from the stove kettle. Then Jo slowly sponged every inch of Zoey, front and back.

Then it was Jo's turn, and she found that she could definitely get used to being so in touch with how her own body looked and felt in Zoey's hands.

Zoey said, "I guess I could live without a shower. Do you think this is how Sandy and Ree stay clean?"

"I dare you to ask them."

They walked over to their hostesses' cabin, comforted in the fact that they had cleaned away any evidence of their lovemaking from the night before and that they were likely to be offered fresh coffee.

As they walked into the "big house," they noticed that it was quite a bit bigger than the guest cabin, and it had an actual upstairs with something in between a ladder and a stairwell joining the two floors.

"Well, it didn't take you two long to settle in, did it?" Sandy chided both of them as they entered.

"Oh, we settled in, all right," Jo said, only to get an elbow in the ribs from Zoey.

"It's only forty miles from Duluth, but it's another world," Zoey mused. She was gawking at the massive log structure. "Is this one of the original homesteads?"

"It is. We feel pretty lucky to have found it. We built the guest cabin and the rest of the outbuildings, but this cabin is original." Sandy led them through the structure and glowed as she told them about her beloved rustic home.

"The logs are tamarack, as are all of the original cabins from the era. This one was built in 1908. The Finlanders who settled here used tamarack because the trees were dying of some tree disease. The Finns are known for their avid environmentalism. It turned out to be a good choice, as you can tell; the logs are still strong." She walked over to touch a log. They all followed suit. "They're scribed to fit together using hand-cut dovetail joints. The joints hold the logs quite well, but they also used sphagnum moss for chinking between the logs—for insulation and to seal the joints." She pointed to a tiny bit of moss visible in a nearby joint.

"Sphagnum moss is still present in the forest today and looks like a green carpet covering the ground. It becomes waterproof when it dries out." She never seemed to lose her delight in talking about the history of the cabin. "We've run across a few other items used to plug holes, such as hankies, socks...even underwear." She raised her eyebrows.

On the walk over, Zoey had noticed a building as large as the size of most two-car garages, built mostly out of slab wood.

"That slab building. It's huge. Is that your woodshed?"

"Yup, the spaces between the slabs serve as draft to dry out the wood, so it can be easily lit and will burn efficiently. That building also houses our four-wheeler with a plow and our garden tractor. We have a separate building—the one closest to your guest cabin—that serves as our garage and shop. We like to call this whole place our 'compound.'"

"You built the screen house and the sauna, too?" Zoey was amazed.

"Don't forget the outhouse."

"Oh, I won't." That brought a laugh to everyone.

"I love the matching green metal roofs. I bet you did that before it was trendy."

"Way before it was trendy."

"We only let friends and family stay in the guest cabin. I think you two fall somewhere in between." That brought smiles all around.

As they settled around the tiny antique kitchen table for a breakfast of sautéed veggies and scrambled eggs, Jo pondered her two loyal and old friends. Having lived in Big Noise, Minnesota, for most of her adult life, Sandy fit the stereotype of a typical local resident, preferring simple country living to plumbing.

Jo mentally took in Sandy across the table from her. *Short, muscle-bound, clothing completely style-free, shaved head. Knows everything about everyone in Big Noise.*

Then she turned her attention to Ree, Sandy's long-term partner, who stood in distinct contrast to Sandy, having dark hair that curled wildly about her face and deep blue eyes uncommon to someone with her dark complexion. Quiet, with a dry sense of humor, Ree moved and lived in a stoic intensity that spoke volumes. Ree was wearing her typical L.L. Bean quick-dry pants and probably a Cabela's catalog fleece shirt. Jo laughed inwardly, thinking about Ree's attempt to drag Sandy to the Twin Cities of Minneapolis and St. Paul to shop for clothes. She had only managed to convince Sandy to add new Carhartt jeans to her wardrobe.

Ree received a significant amount of disposable income as an emergency physician one or two days a week in Two Harbors, so she could afford to indulge Sandy if she had been the least bit interested in new clothing. When Ree wasn't stitching up kids or putting casts on, she ran the ambulance service for Big Noise.

Jo knew from experience after cutting her hand in the kitchen at home and choosing to go to the Two Harbors ER rather than Duluth's (where she would have had to wait hours to be seen) that Ree was a virtual one-stop shop. On top of her dual role of EMT and physician, Ree served on the Volunteer Fire Department, and Sandy had joined, too. Jo imagined the continuity of care possible if you were in need of an ambulance ride to Two Harbors following a minor injury. Ree would arrive on site, do immediate triage, transport her patient to the ER, and then complete her physician's role there.

Jo, who harbored a harmless crush on Ree, smiled at that thought. She wondered silently how things would play out over the next two weeks in such close living arrangements. She also wondered if this little crush would be apparent to Zoey, and whether she would be at all threatened by it. Jo knew that she often had attractions to people that never went anywhere. Could be she was more tuned in to attractions than most.

They all made quick work of the wholesome breakfast. Jo treasured every second with these friends, as she usually saw them only a couple of times a year for any actual quality time.

After the meal, Sandy and Jo joined forces at the cast iron sink to do the dishes while Ree took Zoey on an outdoor tour of the "compound." Sandy had previously heated up well water in a big pot on the stove.

With a big grin, Sandy asked, "So, how are things?"

Playing with her a little, Jo lifted her eyebrows and spread her hands, saying, "What things?"

Sandy tilted her head, smiled, and waited.

Jo laughed out loud, threw her head back and replied, "Incredible."

Sandy nodded and waited until Jo gave in again.

"I'm totally in love. I don't know really how to explain it, but there's no going back. I'm in this. The physical attraction is intense, but there's much more. I've never felt this way before." She looked at Sandy to see if she understood. Sandy nodded.

"I feel so alive. Like I was just going through the motions before. Why didn't you tell me it was like this?"

"That, my friend, is something that you have to learn for yourself. It can't be taught."

"I think I fell so deeply so fast partly because of what we went through together. I mean, we had a near-death experience! We could have been killed. She was right there with me."

"I heard about that. Was it really as scary as the papers said? A gang-hired hit man after you and all that?"

"It was bad. We went hand-to-hand with him. He ended up tracking us to my house, and we lured him into my dark garage and whacked him with a crowbar. Zoey and I worked together. We saved each other's lives. Who knew they made professors like that?"

"Holy shit!" said Sandy. She was shaking her head. It's not that she didn't believe Jo; the tale just seemed so out there.

As they tackled the dishes, Sandy washed, relegating Jo to drying and stacking.

"Well, you sure seem happy and at ease." She gave Jo a wink.

"This has been easier than any relationship I've ever had. But scarier, too. You know, I never really knew what it could be like." Jo was having trouble finding the words to say what she was still working through in her own mind. "I didn't realize how much I kept to myself before and didn't talk about. How it affected things." Jo gestured with the plate she had finished drying. "I think, in part, it's so easy because Zoey doesn't push me and is patient. But caring this much is new and a little frightening. Thankfully, she knows how to put me at ease. She knows when I'm struggling. I feel so safe with her. Safer than I've ever felt with anyone."

"That's great, Jo."

"Actually, I'm planning to ask her to move in with me."

"Wow, that's a breakthrough! Will she say yes?"

"I hope so. I've been the one carrying the baggage."

"Do you have a sense, an intuition? What's your gut telling you?"

"My gut?"

"Yeah, your gut. You're one of the most intuitive people I know, Jo. I don't think you fully understand what you have there." She pointed to her own gut. "You totally underestimate yourself, my big city friend. Is there a little voice that you sometimes listen to that's always right? You know, like feeling an ominous warning, or a good feeling about something that you're facing? I've seen you do it, Jo. You have that ability." She looked at Jo and realized she was striking a nerve, so she went on.

"For me, I have my head, my heart, and my gut." She pointed to each as she referenced them.

"When I'm thinking about something important, I can see it from about eight or nine different perspectives, and talk myself into how each one is right. My head definitely can't get me there. Then there's my heart. I'm a romantic at heart. I want things to come out a certain way, and I can miss the facts in order to fulfill that heartfelt desire." Jo was nodding, recognizing that she had done the same.

"My intuitive voice is right one hundred percent of the time. The trick is that I have to learn to tune into it. Sometimes I fool myself. I think I'm tuned into my gut, but it's my head doing circles around an issue."

Jo nodded enthusiastically. "I know what you mean. I never thought about it like that before. I think I'm more intuitive than anything else, and well, you know about my head. I get stuck in a groove and play things over and over again. Why haven't we had this conversation before? Man, to think of all of the confusion you could have saved me!"

"Well, I think Zoey's great. I'm happy for you."

"Thanks, Sandy."

Changing the subject, Jo asked Sandy if she had heard anything about a Rick Thomas living in the area.

"A friend of yours?"

"Sort of, he was a former client who seems to be missing. Last known location: Big Noise."

"I don't recall hearing anything about him. For sure, we haven't had any report of a missing person at the Rescue Squad. What does he look like?"

"Five-ten, a hundred sixty-five pounds, blondish hair, probably on the long side. He might have been using drugs and hanging out with a young woman."

Jo looked up to see Zoey standing in the doorway.

"What's this about?" Zoey looked mildly concerned.

"It's a guy I know—Rick. He went missing near here. I need to dig into what happened to him. He was one of my kids, you know?"

"One of your kids?"

"He almost feels like a son. I've helped him find jobs, helped him get clean a number of times. He's worked through all of his issues with me over the past eight years. He's a good person normally. Now he's missing, and I need to find him."

Zoey raised her eyebrows. "When did this come up?"

"I got a call from Nate last night when you were asleep." Jo wished she had remembered to mention it before they'd come over to breakfast. If Zoey hadn't been so distracting…

Sandy, watching this interaction, piped up, "Don't forget, you're on vacation."

"Yeah, maybe," Zoey said.

At Jo's stricken look, she sighed and said, "OK, I want to help. What can we do?"

"I don't know what to do, yet. Maybe ask around. See if anyone out here knew him. Nate is checking on things at the PD."

Zoey gave Jo a look that made Jo want to kneel and beg her forgiveness.

Then Zoey said, "It's OK. Your troubled heart is my troubled heart." She grabbed Jo in a big bear hug and gave her a shake.

Chapter 4

DON PACED IN FRONT OF THE WINDOW of their home in Two Harbors. He had come home early from work certain that he would catch his wife, Jean, in bed with another man. He sensed that she was having an affair. He'd been trying to monitor her phone calls and following her from a distance every chance he got. On this day, he told his boss he had a raging headache and needed to use a couple of hours of sick leave. When he got home, she was nowhere in sight. He paced in front of the window for the entire two hours, imagining what she was up to.

When Jean finally pulled into the driveway and into their attached garage, he was waiting for her in the doorway. He felt a little sheepish as she unloaded groceries from her car.

"You OK, Don? You're home early."

"Headache." Don pointed to his head. "I took some ibuprofen. It's easing up."

Headache, right! He's following me. Maybe he'll go to bed early. Maybe I can sneak out and see Frank. God, I feel so trapped. Jean stomped in and out of the house with the groceries.

Why can't we just get a divorce like other normal unhappy couples? Because he's crazy, that's why. He'll kill Frank, and then he'll never let me out of his sight.

She began unpacking the groceries. He was watching her.

He won't even let me have any friends. I miss my friends. I miss my life. Jean felt on the verge of tears, so she went down to the basement to do laundry. She knew it would be too obvious for him to follow her down there.

At least he isn't threatened by my poetry. Thank god for that. I'd be insane without it. She lingered over the laundry as long as she could. She felt like she had to watch every step, or it would all come crashing down on her. He was slowly but surely becoming a monster.

I don't know if I can keep doing this. He's impotent unless he's forcing me to have sex and humiliating me. This is sick! How can I continue to be with him when I love Frank so much? I can't. What can I do? What can I do? I can't go on like this.

Chapter 5

ALTHOUGH ZOEY HAD BEEN WILLING to help Jo look for Rick right away, she seemed happy when Jo said, "No, let's go for a snowshoe," and turning to Sandy and Ree, she asked, "Want to join us?"

"You go ahead and enjoy yourselves," Sandy said. "We have some projects to do. We'll catch up with you later."

Jo and Zoey gathered all of their winterwear and two pairs of snowshoes, and ventured outside the cabin door to the Cloquet River.

After they stepped outside, Jo stood there for a moment. She consciously put her worries about Rick away and let herself live in the moment with Zoey.

"What are you smiling about?" Zoey wanted to know.

Jo felt high. Filled to the brim with being in her element. She was much more at home in the woods than any other place on earth. She so rarely experienced the kind of euphoria she was feeling at that moment. She didn't know if it was how everyone felt when they were in love, but she was soaking it in. All of the colors were a little brighter for her, her sense of taste and smell heightened, every sense on high alert. She didn't have the words to express it, but she hoped that Zoey would understand.

"I feel so good right now. I think it's being in love. I mean, everything is so vivid. I feel so alive." She waved a hand over the river landscape. "Look."

Zoey paused and took in the wilderness tapestry spread out before her. "I feel it, too. I'm glad we came here. I could live like this forever."

They took a moment to lock eyes before beginning their trek. Jo wanted to believe that Zoey was committed enough to accept her totally, including the distractions of her work life. The old Jo would have tried to hide it all. Now, she found herself smiling in spite of her fears.

Jo stood to her full 5-feet, 10-inch height and looked both more relaxed and more alert in that moment than Zoey had ever seen her. Her light blue eyes and white teeth contrasted with her winter tan and short dark hair. Her lean, muscular body was loose but ready for an adventure. Zoey particularly loved seeing that satisfied perma-grin that had taken up residence on Jo's face.

As they traveled slowly down the river, Zoey found that she could maneuver the large old-fashioned snowshoes around downed trees, large boulders, and pockets of open water. For a woman who had moved to northern Minnesota less than six months earlier, she showed no signs of running from the cold and snow. Zoey's bomber-style hat was completely snow covered, and her eyelashes cradled several delicate flakes. Jo watched Zoey as she stopped and looked around with amazement at the beauty of this new place.

In true Zoey fashion, she just had to try her hand at being in the lead, a task usually reserved for experienced river trackers. She struck out confidently, with Jo following close behind. Zoey found that she had an intuitive ability to navigate the frozen river. Jo only had to warn her away from thin ice once.

"You sure you haven't done this before?" Jo asked.

She certainly hadn't gained any of this knowledge in her former home in the New Mexico desert. This terrain was a stark contrast to anything she had ever experienced. Cedar trees grew stubbornly out of rock formations bordering the river. A snowy blanket covered many large white pine branches that hovered over them. Their breathing produced short bursts of steam.

Jo's loyal pups, Java and Cocoa, seemed to be enjoying the freedom of this vacation as well. Rarely staying on trail throughout the snowshoe, they jumped through snow up to their ears for jaunts up the riverbank in search of real and imagined animals to capture. Zoey knew from experience that large animals or anything that would give them chase would land them squarely underfoot in search of mom's protection. Zoey realized suddenly that she had already grown attached to these impetuous dogs.

While Zoey was dressed perfectly for the snowshoe hike, she also knew that she presented herself as somewhat of a geek. All of her clothes were too new, and she was too well put together to look natural. When she made the move up north, she hadn't owned any jackets heavier than a light windbreaker. She had acquired quite a bit of gear since then, but she hadn't yet adjusted to the casual way most northerners cared for their outerwear. She rarely wore anything twice without washing it. She flashed on the memory of the day Jo caught her ironing her flannel shirts. Jo had chuckled as she gently pointed out that if she was going to iron flannel, she better not leave a crease or everyone would know.

She wondered if she was really cut out for this adventure in the woods with no washing machine or iron. Zoey reflected on how opposite she and Jo were in so many ways. Regarding their clothes, they were like north to south, yin to yang. Jo appeared to care little for what she wore. She donned virtually the same outfit every day for work or play: one of her twelve button-down Pendleton shirts with one of the dozen pairs of permanent-press, khaki pants she owned. When her work clothing became worn, she rotated it into her casual clothing. Zoey did notice, however, that Jo had brought along some fleece shirts and pants in anticipation of their rustic adventure. That totally cracked her up.

Where the river narrowed for a curve, they found themselves nearly encircled in snow-covered branches. Zoey knew from experience not to stand under them, as it would afford her lover the opportunity to give one of them a shove, causing snow to fall on her head and down her neck.

As they entered a clearing with no trees overhead, Zoey slowed, moved in a large circle, and turned to face Jo. She inched her snowshoes in closer, placing one in between Jo's legs and the other to one side, and leaned in. She knew Jo couldn't possibly move now, without toppling both of them over into a snowshoe/human heap.

Zoey gave Jo a wicked little grin and moved in for a kiss. She could feel Jo smiling as those warm lips melted into her own. Jo gave in easily and fully to Zoey, and Zoey could tell that Jo's entire body was warming over with pleasure. Jo let out a laugh after the kiss.

"What?" Zoey inquired.

"I could take you again right here." Jo was still laughing.

"You really can't get enough, can you?"

"I'm smitten. What can I say? I love seeing you out here. It totally does me in." Jo flicked a little snow off of Zoey's hat before they started back toward the cabin.

The warmth of that kiss easily lasted for the mile-long return hike.

Chapter 6

DON HAD FINISHED BRINGING the last of the supplies out to his bunker. He felt so satisfied with his work. Here he had control of everything. Here everything was perfect. In the real world, so many people were always fucking up his plans. It felt good to be able to control everything about this place.

As he relaxed at the thought of his safe bunker, he heard in his mind his father's harsh words: "You stupid idiot! Why do you have to wreck everything?"

He was sitting in a boat the one time when they had tried to go fishing together. He had been so happy when his father offered to take him. Just the two of them. They didn't do things together like the other ten-year-old boys in his school did with their fathers. He wanted so badly for his father to be proud of him and to want to spend time with him.

Sitting in that boat, he could see it all falling apart. He had tangled his line with his father's. He'd also gotten it wrapped around the propeller of the motor. He felt helpless as his father angrily tried to untangle the mess. He could feel his father's rage mounting. Not only was the fishing trip over, but he would get a sound beating before they even made it back to the car.

He fought back the urge to cry. To cry now would only result in a more immediate beating. He began counting the number of rivets holding the three sections of the boat bottom together. By the time he got to thirty-seven, he realized that his father was yelling at him again.

"Donald. Are you listening to me?"

Donald looked up. He had made another terrible mistake. "Yes, sir."

"Then what did I just say?"

"Dad, I'm sorry. I don't remember."

"Then you lied to me, didn't you?"

"I didn't try to."

"Come here."

Donald was frozen. He knew his father was going to hit him, so he couldn't move. One day, he was going to fight back. He would become strong enough so that his father would never even think about hitting him. One day, his dad would pay for beating him like this. He knew that other boys weren't beaten like he was.

He cursed himself for being so stupid. Why couldn't he stop screwing things up?

The boat rocked from side to side as his father got to his feet and moved toward him. A strong arm grabbed him as another one cracked him on the side of his head.

His father slowly made his way back to the rear of the boat before speaking.

"Don't lie to me."

Donald knew that even if he had been honest about not hearing his father, he would have been hit for not listening. He felt what would become for him the familiar feeling of helpless paralysis about how to behave in his father's presence.

Chapter 7

AFTER THEIR SNOWSHOE, Jo and Zoey followed Sandy to the post office for her afternoon shift (this branch of the U.S. Postal Service apparently had rather limited hours, as Sandy was the only employee). They were curious to see where she worked. Before entering, Sandy chatted with a couple of waiting customers as she unlocked the crude padlock protecting the tiny post office from would-be burglars. As she entered the customer area that housed two chairs and no room for a line, she asked the customers to hold off on coming in until she could open the inner door to her service counter. The door opened out, and if they came into the building with her, there wouldn't be enough room to open the door.

Once at her station, she turned up the heat and used her key to open the cash register. She had a four-hour shift ahead of her, and she hoped it would be a busy one. If the waiting customers were any indication, she thought she might get her wish. When things got slow, she had to do online data entry, a task she did not enjoy.

After she had served her first several customers, she brewed a pot of coffee, pouring cups for everyone.

"So, how'd you get to be postmistress?" Zoey inquired.

"Well, the previous one—Mabel Swenson—retired two years ago. They put an ad in the paper, and I was the only one to apply." Sandy shrugged. "The old post office was in Mabel's garage. When I was offered the job, it was under the condition that I either build a new one or oversee the new construction. I'm pretty sure they banked on me wanting to build it myself."

Sandy looked around at the snug structure with pride. "I added it onto the fire hall. There were some funny code requirements, though. Studs had to be six inches apart. The walls a foot thick. Don't want anyone breaking in to steal the mail."

Ten customers and an hour later, Sandy had a break of about fifteen minutes. "When I first took this job, I envisioned myself reading novels or catching up on my correspondence. No way is that going to happen. I have to inventory, fill out online forms, etcetera. For such a small operation, there's a lot of busy work."

They heard a car pulling into the parking lot. Sandy could see through the small window on the door that it was an Explorer, driven by Jean Anderson, whose mailing address was in Two Harbors. Sandy couldn't really figure out why Jean did so much of her mailing business in Big Noise. Once Sandy processed Jean's package and the woman got into her car, Sandy turned back to Zoey and Jo.

"That is one troubled woman. Hangs out at G's Café and reads poetry. Her writing is dark. From what I heard in her poems, she's married to a sick, controlling bastard. She seemed lonely, so I kept trying to draw her out. There's a certain vulnerability to her."

"And?" They all knew Sandy had more.

"And she's working up to leave him. I think she's seeing someone up here. Why else would she drive all the way from Two Harbors to mail her packages?"

"Do you think it's a woman?" Jo's eyebrows shot up.

"I doubt it. Didn't get that vibe from her. She's scared shitless of the husband, though."

"Women are at the highest risk of abuse when they leave. I specialized in domestic violence offenders for years," Jo said.

"Well, I hope that doesn't play out up here," Sandy said.

"Abusers get off on the control they can exert over their victims," Zoey added. "But they're hurting themselves, really. Someone taught them that they have to maintain power to survive. They need help, and if they can get that help, we're all a little safer."

Chapter 8

THE SAUNA WAS HOT, and Jo found it hard to understand how her friends could stand the heat. After they all stripped off their clothes and settled in, a wash of sadness and anxiety must have shown on her face as she looked at her friend Sandy's scarred breast area. Sandy must have sensed her feelings and spoke to relieve some of the tension.

"I kind of like the scars. It makes me feel like a survivor, you know," she said as she looked down at her own chest.

Jo had gone to see Sandy in the hospital when she underwent a double mastectomy. She had also been there when Sandy decided against reconstruction. Sandy's justification was that she didn't want a longer recovery time but also because they would place the breast augmentation under her pectoral muscles. She feared it would impact her strength—the strength she so needed to do the construction work she loved. At just under five feet, she needed all of the strength available to her. Jo moved to a lower bench so that she could tolerate the heat enough to continue their conversation.

"So what does your doctor say? Have you had more follow-up visits since we last talked?"

"Still all clear. No reoccurrence." As Sandy said it, she crossed her fingers.

"And are you back to full strength? It's been, what, eight months?"

"Ten actually, and I feel great. They didn't take any muscle, so I'm feeling as good as new."

"Has it changed you at all? You know, facing a cancer scare like that?"

"Well, I think I'm even more grateful that I only work part time. I have time to really enjoy life, Ree, the people I care about. I think it reaffirmed for me that I'm living my life the way I want to."

Jo felt an instinctive need to touch Sandy's scars, but she held back the urge. They looked like smiles. Somehow being close friends with a lesbian added more rigid boundaries. She wondered if she would hold back that urge if they were heterosexual friends. Instead, she reached for Sandy's hand and gave it a tug. This small gesture captured more than either one of them could have put into words.

Jo only lasted a short time before wandering out into the cool winter air. Every inch of her steamed as her body temp. came back down to a comfortable level. Inside, she could hear murmurs of a conversation about the Big Noise Fire Department. She was sure Zoey was full of questions, and she made a mental note to ask Sandy and Ree for a tour of the fire hall and trucks before the vacation ended. She had her hopes up about getting a ride in the fire truck. She had heard that Sandy had been assigned to run the engine/pumper. That was no small feat, given Sandy's height, but Jo was picturing it as she steamed outside the sauna. She imagined Sandy sitting in the truck on top of a phone book, steering the big rig.

Outside of the hot sauna, the wind had picked up a bit. The trees behind her were creaking in their effort to resist the blasts. Little swirls of snow rose and then died down in the opening between the sauna and the cabin. Jo knew that she never would have noticed such simple beauty before falling in love with Zoey. She breathed in the deep scent of winter and then stepped back into the sauna.

The rest of the group stayed inside for forty minutes. They finished by showering inside the sauna with a big warm bucket and a pitcher. When it was Zoey's turn, Jo poured the water for her. "You will never be cleaner than after a sauna."

"So, this is the secret? We do this every day?"

Everyone laughed. "Once or twice a week," Ree volunteered, looking apologetic. Apparently, she had still not quite adjusted to this lifestyle herself.

Zoey managed a weak smile.

"I'll see what we can do about keeping you clean." Jo was thinking about their earlier sponge bath, and she flashed Zoey a grin.

"Get a room, girls!" Sandy complained. "Oh, that's right, you already have one. Disregard," she added, with a dismissive wave of her hand.

Chapter 9

THEY GATHERED AROUND A TABLE in front of the woodstove for a full night of poker. Jo's eyes wandered about the cabin, taking in the uniqueness of it as they played. Perhaps that contributed to her demise as a poker player. There were coats, hats, long underwear, and all sorts of things hanging about, presumably to dry out. Sandy and Ree had hand-crafted custom nooks and crannies to hold mittens and kitchen things. All were designed to blend into the log cabin theme while maintaining the whole rustic atmosphere.

They played "winner calls the game and winner deals." Sandy must have dealt over half of the hands and was hooting and hollering after every win. She would start in, and they'd all follow. Each time their voices rose, Cocoa would get up and go over to Jo to see if she was all right, and then look outside to see if they were yelling because someone had arrived. Once she was certain there was nothing to guard them from, she would settle down in front of the fire and begin to sleep. When the next hand ended, the whole thing would start again.

By the end of the night, Jo was down four bucks, and Zoey was down two. Jo teased, "No wonder our rent is so cheap. I smell a scam."

As Jo and Zoey left for the guest cabin, Ree turned to Sandy and said, "Remember when we were so new? We used to look at each other like that. I think we were every bit as hot for each other as they are." They watched Jo and Zoey holding hands as they walked away.

Sandy looked at Ree and said, "Of course I remember. We still have some fun once in a while, and after fifteen years, that's pretty good."

Ree had moved closer to Sandy and put her arm around her. "Especially on date night."

Sandy slid her hand under Ree's shirt and felt the warm skin of her back. "And on other nights." She gave her a little nudge toward the stairway. "What do you say we get naked and see what happens?"

Ree's expression, which Sandy could read without fail after all their years together, was in the affirmative. Sandy pulled her toward the stairway. Once they reached the top of the stairs, Ree turned to Sandy, picked her up, hoisted her over her shoulder, and not so gently, deposited her on the bed. She stood over her, waiting for a response.

"Oh, you big butch, I could do that to you, too, you know."

"I have a lot of other moves you've never seen," Ree said.

"Well then, we have that much more to look forward to."

Ree got a serious look on her face, so Sandy settled down and faced her on her side. "What, hon?"

Ree drew a picture of a heart over Sandy's scarred breast area, over her actual heart. "Love is like a heartbeat, you know."

Sandy scrunched up her nose. "A heartbeat? Is this like a doctor thing? 'Cause we can play that game, if you like," Sandy teased.

"You know, like a heart monitor where you can see your heart beating. There's a baseline, then a peak, then it drops below the baseline, and then again back up. The baseline is when we met. We didn't know if we would be friends or lovers. Then we peaked for a few years until around year seven, maybe eight. Then we dropped down below. Remember? We didn't even notice." Sandy realized Ree was being serious and nodded.

"Then one day you said, 'Hon, what happened to us? Did we consciously stop having sex?'" I was a little perturbed at you at first because I was watching *Northern Exposure*. Like it was the most important thing in the world. You waited for the show to end and said, 'I think we need to set up a date night. I want us to keep our passion alive.' Remember that?" Sandy smiled back at Ree and nodded yes.

"So, that's how it started, and ever since we've been going strong, with our own little rhythm. Once a week, we have a romantic, sit-down dinner, watch a movie, get naked, and sometimes we end up asleep, or laughing, or we make love." Ree paused, and Sandy smiled at her and stroked her cheek.

She was touched by how this had meant so much to Ree.

"I think I know how to bring us back up to baseline tonight, sweetie. I might even try for a few peaks." Ree's eyes had smoked over with desire, so Sandy took her into her arms and kissed her deeply. Ree relaxed into Sandy's embrace, finding that they still fit together like an old shoe. She knew exactly where all of their curves came together. She moved against Sandy and reached to find her clit. She began making slow circles with her hand while moving against her.

Sandy was so stirred by Ree's earnestness about keeping their passion alive that she quickly found herself moving toward orgasm.

As Sandy arched up, Ree backed off a little bit, and whispered into her ear, "I love you more than ever." Then she slowly shifted lower and made circular motions with her tongue until she heard Sandy cry out and felt her melt. She moved up quickly and took Sandy in her arms, holding her close.

"That was quick." Ree didn't want to spoil the moment, but she was feeling an urgent need herself. She managed to wait until she felt Sandy's heart slow.

Sandy looked at Ree. "What do you need, hon?"

Ree's answer was to guide Sandy's hand down until she was inside her. Sandy moved her body in unison with her hand until she could feel Ree's arousal. She slowed her thrusts a bit, looked into Ree's eyes, and said, "I love you more than ever, too, my Ree." As she said it, Ree tumbled into orgasm.

"Hold me."

"I am."

"Closer."

Sandy couldn't imagine how they could be closer, but she placed her cheek against Ree's and allowed her emotions to wash over and through her. She knew that because Ree was so quiet, only letting others into her world through her dry humor, her lover was the only person in the world to know this serious and intense side of her. After they held each other for a time, Ree backed up a bit, looked into Sandy's eyes, and said, "We found some peaks tonight."

"That we did."

Ree moved in behind Sandy and pressed her nose and lips against Sandy's warm neck, taking in her scent.

"I love falling asleep surrounded by the smell of our sex."
"Mmmm. Me, too."

Back in the guest cabin, Jo and Zoey stoked the fire with an all-night log, nearly closed the damper for a slow burn, and climbed up into the loft. They had to open a window to cool it down enough to sleep. The walls of the loft were cedar and emitted a distinctive aroma. The bed was a simple futon mattress placed directly on the floor. The ceiling of the loft was only five feet above the bed. Two pine dressers with a hand-built open closet standing in between were all that the space contained. The floor of pine boards was left unfinished. The space was cozy without feeling tight. They lay in silence for a minute reflecting on the day before Zoey turned to Jo.

"Jo."

Jo leaned on an elbow and looked at Zoey. She seemed to need the intimacy and recognition, so Jo waited until she went on.

"I really did a good thing moving here. I love all of it. You, this incredible extended community, the outdoors. I had no idea."

"I'm the lucky one. What did you think it would be like?"

"I don't know. I mean, I thought it would be good. I love the outdoors. I guess I never expected to meet so many great people. I mean you, our Valley community, now these two. I love it all."

"You like these guys?"

"They're the best. They seem so happy and at ease with their lives, with each other. That Ree, what a hoot! She seems so serious, and then she hits you with her dry humor."

"They are great. Sandy and I have been friends for a long time. We've only been able to see each other a couple of times a year lately, but it's always easy. Comfortable. I'm a lucky girl."

"Yes, my dear, you are."

Zoey leaned in and finished the kiss she had started on the river. Their kisses had become longer and less urgent as time passed, but no less intense. Jo reflected in her mind that their kisses had evolved from an exclamation point to a paragraph and now sometimes to an entire chapter. She had begun to feel like Zoey was a part of her. Jo felt relaxed from the sauna and the poker game. She pulled Zoey's arm around her tighter. As she did, Java let out a moan down below. Jo ignored her jealous boy and found herself wondering how Sandy's brush with cancer had affected Sandy and Ree's relationship. She suspected that it had only brought them closer together. She was smiling at that as she felt herself drift off into sleep.

Chapter 10

ALTHOUGH HE HAD BEEN walking for hours, and his legs felt tired, he continued. He felt strong when he pushed himself beyond what others could do. The crisp winter air felt good, and it had suited his purpose that the snow was firm underfoot as he crunched along. Up ahead of him was a trail. It was clearly a human trail as opposed to a deer trail because of the still-distinguishable boot marks present. His heart beat faster as he followed the trail.

Soon a shack took form in the woods. It wasn't much of a shack. More like slab wood covered in tarpaper. He approached slowly and silently. He stopped and sniffed the air and listened for any signs of life. Once he determined that all was quiet, he moved slowly up to the door. Again he stood quietly and listened for sounds. Hearing none, he banged on the door with his shotgun. Nothing stirred.

He pushed open the flimsy plywood and waited another moment before walking into the cramped, dark space. Once his eyes adjusted to the lack of light, he could see that the shack was stuffed full of car stereos, flat-screen TVs, and DVD/DVR players. He jumped to the conclusion that they must be stolen.

He felt strength gather in him because he was going to right this wrong.

He immediately got to work. He brought all of the items outside one by one and lined them up on the ground. After retrieving an axe from a nearby stump, he smashed each and every item until it was unusable. He had never felt so useful and fulfilled.

Once his work on the electronics was done, he took the small structure down with the axe as well. He was totally exhausted by the time he began the long walk back to his bunker.

As Don walked, he realized that he had been so lost in thought that he didn't know if he was moving in the right direction or not. He kept going for another fifteen minutes without seeing one of the crosses that would tell him which direction to go. Thoughts of self-doubt crept into his head, sounding very much like his father's voice.

"Stupid idiot. Why don't you pay attention?"

"No, I'm not stupid. I righted a wrong. I broke their stolen stuff."

He sat down and went through all of his walking in his mind. When he was really stressed, he replayed things over and over again.

When he felt calm enough, Don made a huge cross from two downed trees and laid it down flat on the ground so that he wouldn't mistake it for one that would show him the way to his bunker. When he was finished, his stress level had reduced enough for him to begin walking again. After another twenty minutes, he came across a directional marker. He quickened his pace and followed it with the zeal of a hunting hound. When he finally made it back to his safe place, he was totally exhausted.

Chapter 11

TYPICALLY A FITFUL SLEEPER, Jo found that this night was no exception. Just before waking, Jo dreamed that she was walking through the woods on snowshoes at dawn. The trail she was on had been previously snowshoed and was firmly packed. There were boot tracks as well on the trail, and she couldn't figure out who they belonged to. As she walked, she felt that someone was watching her.

When she turned around, she sensed rather than saw someone or something darting behind trees. She started walking again and quickly turned around in an attempt to see who was following and watching her. She did this several times before yelling, "Who are you?" Several clients inched out from behind the trees. They all opened their mouths to speak.

Before hearing what they wanted, she woke up. Jo sat up and rubbed her eyes, thinking, *Man, I did need this vacation.*

In her job, she was literally at the beck and call of parents, clients, police, and all of the PO's in her unit. An answering service fielded calls twenty-four hours a day. The service attempted to reach the Probation Officer assigned to the caller. If the service couldn't reach the PO, they forwarded the call to Jo. Often the caller was requesting permission to go out of town, or parents were having trouble with their child and were seeking guidance. More often than not, a frustrated parent or foster parent wanted the officer to lock up the youth for minor infractions. Jo looked out the window into the blackness and pondered why the stress of her job had found its way into the serenity she could almost always rediscover when she was in the woods.

That led to Jo thinking about her missing former client Rick. OK, what did she know that she could use as a starting point? He had been in the Big

Noise area and was likely doing something illegal. According to the teenage runaway who had been hanging out with him, he was using drugs again.

Reflecting back on their relationship, she knew that his pattern was to call her when he was clean, looking for advice or to hear an encouraging word from her. If he was indeed using drugs again, it was typical that he hadn't called.

Jo normally would have tracked him down by now if she hadn't been preoccupied by her developing relationship with Zoey. Now she worried that the oversight might have been a costly one.

When Rick was clean, she took him out to lunch once in a while to try to encourage him to stay that way. And when he was too far down to help himself, she would go looking for him and haul him into detox to help him get back to sobriety again. Jo had long-term relationships with a few of her other former clients, but she recognized that she had a particular soft spot for Rick.

She smiled to herself as she thought about his fondness for dogs. When Rick was clean, he spent time volunteering at the animal shelter caring for homeless dogs. Jo had even allowed him to help her train Cocoa when she was a pup. Even to this day, she had to be careful when mentioning his name around Cocoa or she would run to the door eager to see him. It made Jo's heart ache thinking about him being out of touch for so long. Not just out of touch with her, but out of touch period.

Even though not calling her was an indication that he might be hiding out until he could present himself more favorably, her gut was telling her that he wasn't in the area, or that he was dead. She resolved to do what she could to find Rick out here, or find out where he'd gone. Otherwise, she would always wonder why she hadn't tried to help him when he was in trouble. Both she and Nate suspected that he had stumbled into something bad.

She knew that she wouldn't get back to sleep easily, so she padded down the ladder and into the cabin kitchen. She opened the freezer and pulled out a quart-sized container of ice cream. Eating ice cream in the middle of the night was a bad habit, but it seemed to help her relax. She spooned a couple of scoops into a bowl and then set it down for a few minutes on the woodstove. Just as a puddle was developing in the bottom of the bowl, she picked it up, sat on the floor in front of the fire with her back to the couch, and dug into the soft treat.

The moon shone in through a window behind her, and between the moonlight and the flames from the fire, she could clearly see her two dogs sitting patiently at her side waiting to find out if they would get to lick the bowl when she was done. Even though she couldn't sleep, she found quite a bit of serenity in her wakefulness.

"Hon, you OK?" Zoey managed in a sleepy voice.

"I'm OK. I'll be up in a minute."

"Eating ice cream?"

Jo laughed. "Want some?"

"Bad dream?"

"Not too bad. It was about work. I'll tell you in the morning. Go back to sleep. I'm fine."

"'Night, hon."

Jo felt herself smile at this simple interchange. *Yup, she was a keeper.*

Chapter 12

SANDY AND REE AWOKE early the next morning. Their lovemaking had left a warm, fuzzy feeling with both of them. The sun was peaking over the horizon.

"It's good to see Jo so happy, isn't it?" Ree said into the back of Sandy's neck.

Turning over, Sandy responded, "Yeah, it really is. I think they're a good match. Zoey seems stable. It's going to be fun watching who Jo is in this relationship."

Ree nodded in her quiet way, knowing that Sandy had more to say.

"It was so frustrating to see her try and force things with Dar. I mean, she had to bend way too far to be with her. I never got that, did you?"

Ree shook her head no. "Not unless you're attracted to the f'd up artist type," she said with a small smile. She then traced a line down Sandy's jawline with her index finger.

"Yeah," Sandy continued, "the tension between them became unbearable. I can't imagine Jo coming home to that, given how stressful her job is. Zoey seems centered, like she knows who she is. I'm actually kind of shocked at how good they seem together."

Ree nodded in agreement, yawned, and pulled Sandy closer to her, placing Sandy's head under her chin, and then said, "Much like we do, my dear."

Sandy gave her a little elbow before turning and snuggling back into the comfortable spoon they had grown so accustomed to over the years. "It's going to be fun having them hang around for a couple of weeks."

Ree didn't respond, and Sandy knew that her lover had fallen back to sleep. She soon joined her.

Morning for Jo and Zoey brought coffee from a stovetop percolator and teeth brushing with cold well water poured from a five-gallon jug. Zoey didn't complain and settled into the loft with some work while Jo planned to head off to the big house to see if anyone wanted to join her for a morning ski or snowshoe. Zoey chose to stay behind this time, but said. "Hey, when you get back, there's something I want to talk to you about."

Jo nodded, "Sure, hon," before heading out the door. Jo didn't have any kind of gauge here and found herself wondering what this conversation would be about. *Maybe she hates cabin life. Or maybe she's going to suggest that she move in with me. That would be just like her, to beat me to the punch. We are so in sync with each other.*

Sandy was building a shelf unit in her shop, but Ree jumped at the chance for a ski. "Heck, yeah. Thanks for tracking the river. Let's grab our skis and see how far you got."

Jo took both dogs. Once they saw her grab her skis, stowed in the cabin's porch, she knew she couldn't possibly leave them with Zoey or they would whine and cry the entire time she was gone. Besides, they were used to their habitual morning trail time with Jo, so it would have been cruel to deny them. Even when Jo was involved in a case that was at a critical stage, she tried to stick to her routines. It kept her centered and sometimes led to her best problem solving.

On the river, Jo was awestruck by the silence. The day was sunny, and the sky a light blue.

She and Ree could see their breath, but the sun felt warm on their faces. They quickly traversed the one mile of tracked river and proceeded onward, taking turns tracking the deep snow for another mile on skis. The going was slow, and Jo quickly worked up a sweat. By the end of the second mile, Jo was skiing in only a fleece shirt, with her jacket tied around her waist.

Ree had also stripped off her outer layer about ten minutes before, and Jo noticed Ree's athletic physique beneath her wool sweater and long-underwear shirt. She was amused by the fact that she had been naked in the sauna with her the night before and hadn't even looked at her at all. Ree caught her looking and turned her head to one side. "What? Never seen a blue-eyed Inuit before?"

Cocoa had built up snowballs on his underside and was stopping frequently to try to chew them off, so Jo used the opportunity to stop and lean down to work on some of the snowballs, thereby skillfully avoiding looking at Ree. Java immediately moved over to sit by Ree because he was used to the ritual of snow removal on his brother. His short hair never iced up on his belly or in between his toes.

"Inuit?"

"I have quite a bit of Alaskan Inuit blood in me. Native Alaskan. If you went there, you'd be amazed. Blue eyes are rare, though, and actually, curly hair is unheard of. I'm also quite a bit taller than any Inuit I've ever met."

Jo chuckled and said, "No, I never have seen a blue-eyed Inuit until now. Are they all as striking as you?" As soon as she said it, she felt herself blush. If she was lucky, the sun and heat from skiing would hide the redness.

"The Inuit are a very distinct people, and thank you. I don't think I've ever been called striking before."

"I didn't mean to make you uncomfortable."

"No, not at all." She smiled a big smile that said, *Don't worry, I like being cute.*

Jo found herself wondering what this interchange was about. She found Ree attractive, but it was a surface crush. She knew she had even experienced this appreciation with some men. It never went beyond that. She knew this to be true and found herself relaxing a bit. Jo suspected that Ree had dealt with this before. She looked back at Jo in her quiet way and continued petting Java.

"Feel like turning back?" Jo offered.

"Let's do it."

The ski back was fast and wordless; the quiet sound of their skis slicing through the snow hypnotic and relaxing. By the end of the ski, Jo was in one of those rare athletic zones that you hear about, high on exercise and endorphins. After depositing Ree back at the big house, Jo quickly made her way back to the guest cabin.

Chapter 13

AFTER JO AND REE LEFT for their ski, Zoey had begun working on preparing her syllabus for one of her next classes. She loved the work, but she was also glad she didn't have to do much preparation during this vacation She was looking forward to spending time with Jo, Sandy, and Ree.

She pondered her move to Duluth. While the career change was just what she needed, she hadn't expected to be lucky enough to move right into a tight-knit community of lesbians. She had left behind many friends, and from time to time, that did tug on her heart.

The driving force in her career change had been that even in a city the size of Albuquerque, she was constantly running into patients. She didn't feel that she had a life outside of work. Going to a play, the mall, or even a basketball game meant running into people with whom she was ethically unable to socialize, and she often had to deal with uncomfortable situations. On top of that, although she felt that she was a successful therapist and that she had done some good work, she was beginning to feel worn down by patients who really didn't want to change. Many of them would come into therapy and expect the problems to go away because they were talking about them.

The challenge of leaving behind everything she knew and starting fresh had turned out to be a cleansing experience. It wasn't that she had run from her past; she had consciously decided to begin building a new life.

Zoey realized that she hadn't been focusing on the syllabus and gave herself permission to set it aside. She got up from the table, poured herself a cup of coffee, and sat down in front of the fire. Although she was head over heels in love with Jo, some of Jo's bad habits were definitely wearing off on her. Coffee caused her the most concern. She had become accustomed to having coffee ready for Jo whenever they were together, and over time, her own consumption rate had gradually increased. During this two-week vacation, it could become problematic, as the only bathroom was an unheated outhouse. She would have to make a conscious effort to cut back on coffee. Right after this cup.

Zoey found that she was missing Cocoa and Java. They knew just how to get her to give them an extra treat when Jo wasn't around. Cocoa had taken to sleeping at her feet when she was reading or working. Often she would reach down and scratch her ears as she worked through a question or problem in her mind. When she was at home alone, she often found herself missing all of them, Jo included.

She mused that one of the things she loved most about Jo was her loyalty to her friends and coworkers. Zoey also enjoyed the fun they had in the out of doors. Jo's passion for nature, combined with her love of skiing, hiking, and snowshoeing made the two of them a perfect fit. Zoey had played sports in high school and college, but she'd never had a partner who could show her how great outdoor recreation could be until she'd met Jo.

One thing bothered her, though. She was concerned about Jo's intense job and how dangerous it could be. She knew that Jo would risk her life for something or someone she cared about. It was a quality that she respected and feared in Jo. She didn't quite know what to do with the possibility of losing her. She imagined the future as many nights sitting home waiting and wondering if Jo was in danger.

This might be even more stressful if they lived together. She wondered if the plans she was making would sit well with Jo. Although Zoey craved every second she could spend with her lover, she knew that Jo needed a home life that was orderly, uncomplicated, and a refuge from her work. Zoey didn't want to intrude on that. She felt that she could easily wait to make sure they were both ready before they moved in together.

Jo was so incredibly good and so brave. Too brave. She seemed to think that saving the world was in her job description. But she had a fragile side to her as well. She beat herself up too much when anything went wrong in her relationships. Like most sensitive people do, Zoey reflected.

She sometimes worried about Jo's process for dealing with decisions surrounding intimacy. She knew Jo had a tendency to be overly self-critical. She hoped she would work through the change she was about to suggest without torturing herself too much. Jo wasn't nearly as screwed up about relationships as she thought she was.

Zoey smiled at the thought of Jo and found that the ever-so-light, musky smell of her lover lingered in the cabin. She picked up one of Jo's shirts that was hanging on a hook, breathed in her scent, smiled again. *Damn, this was going to be hard.*

Chapter 14

WHEN JO GOT BACK from her ski, she found Zoey puttering around in the cabin kitchen making soup. Jo knew without asking that it was potato garlic with bacon, and the aroma was almost too much for her to take. She was starving.

She walked up behind Zoey and nibbled on her ear. "Mmm. I'm not sure who smells better, or is enticing me more, you or this soup. It smells fantastic."

Zoey turned around, pulling Jo into her. "Oh, I smell as good as garlic now, do I? Well, from now on, I'll put a little behind my ears since you seem so fond of it." Zoey closed her eyes and placed her cheek against Jo's, taking in a more potent version of her lover's scent. She felt so at home with the intensity and comfort of their embrace. She marveled at how they fit together so perfectly. Being in Jo's arms felt like being at home.

"Let's talk over lunch, OK?" She felt Jo stiffen slightly and found herself laughing. "It's nothing bad, hon; I'd just like to share some news."

"I see you're buttering me up with soup." Jo continued to hold Zoey, savoring the feel of her soft cheek. She couldn't help but want to expose more skin to enjoy.

Zoey had made a loaf of Irish soda bread to go along with the soup. Once they were settled at the table, Zoey knew she had to get the conversation going. Jo was so tense she was hardly eating. And oh, how Zoey loved to watch Jo devour food she had cooked for her.

"OK, here's what I wanted to tell you." She looked at her to make sure Jo was paying attention. Jo nodded weakly.

"You know how close my rental house is to the university?" Jo nodded.

"Well, the university wants to build a dorm right there. They're buying the whole block. My landlord is terminating my lease early. It's not so bad, really. He's giving me a tidy sum for the inconvenience." Jo relaxed a bit. *This would be the perfect time.*

"I found a condo in the west hillside area that I really like. I want you to come and take a look at it, see what you think." She looked at Jo expectantly, but said, "It will be a little further away from work, but it will be better than renting. I can do what I want with the place. The best part is that all the exterior maintenance will be taken care of. I'll have more time to spend with you at your place, mowing or whatever."

A wave of simultaneous thoughts overcame Jo: *She's not even considering the idea of moving in with me. She must not think it would work out. So much for my vast powers of intuition.*

She sat there, her mind a buzzing whirr, and finally managed to say, "Yes, I can see how that might work well." For once, Jo wasn't thrilled with the attention Zoey was paying to her every expression. *She's a therapist. What does she think is wrong with me? Maybe all my talk about Dar has convinced her that living with me would be a disaster. I have totally screwed this up.*

Zoey reached across the table and took Jo's hand.

"What's wrong? I can see you're upset." Jo wouldn't look at her. "Were you thinking that you wanted me to move in with you?"

"Sometime, yes. But I can see you're obviously not sure about it."

"Oh, no, Jo. I just think we should take things slow. I still have two months before I have to be out. We have time before making a decision."

"But, why? I'm feeling ready to share my life with you, but you're pulling back."

"That's not true. You may think you're ready, but I don't want anything to destroy what we're building. I've seen too many couples make quick decisions that end up dooming their relationship. It's important not to rush things."

"You still haven't told me why you think we need to wait."

"I guess I've assumed you need your own space. You are kind of compulsive." She noticed Jo's shoulders start to slump, and hurriedly added, "I can handle that. But the thing that I'm not sure about is your inclination to put yourself in danger—trying to make everything right in the world, almost all by yourself."

"But that's who I am. If you want me to change, tell me what you need me to do."

"It's not that I want you to change, just be more careful. And I want us to take things a little slower."

"But buying a condo? That's pretty permanent." Jo's heart felt like it was straining through her chest wall. She rubbed her upper chest, trying to calm herself down.

"I want to wait until you're sure you're ready."

"You're the one who's not ready." Jo pushed back her chair and got abruptly to her feet.

"Jo, wait!"

But Jo had already left the cabin.

Chapter 15

ZOEY QUICKLY FOLLOWED her outside with Jo's coat in her hand, saying, "You're going to need this," further embarrassing Jo.

Sandy came trotting over to them before they could say anything more, greeting them with her usual enthusiasm.

"Hurry up, girls! Get some coffee into you, 'cuz Amanda needs us. I hope you've eaten something, too. It's gonna be hard work."

Jo stammered, "What?"

"Amanda just left. A tree fell on her house last night. She has a hole the size of a car in her roof. We gotta help!" She gave Jo a curious look. "You do want to help, don't you?"

Jo finally looked at Zoey and shrugged her shoulders. "Yeah, sure."

Zoey said, "I guess this is all part of the Big Noise experience, isn't it?" Jo just shook her head.

It took five minutes for them to get to Amanda's driveway and another ten to snowshoe in to her cabin. Jo found herself wondering how Amanda could quickly respond as a volunteer firefighter under those conditions. She also wondered how Amanda kept up with bringing in groceries throughout the winter. She had been to Amanda's in summer and knew that she pulled right up to her cabin once it was dry enough to drive in. Maybe she used a sled.

The entire group alternately traded off carrying two backpacks filled with tools. Thankfully, Amanda had enough wood on hand for the repairs because Jo couldn't contemplate having to drive into Duluth or Two Harbors to get supplies and then bring them into Amanda's property by sled. It was really starting to hit home with her how difficult living out in the boonies could be. She was also amazed at how tight-knit the community was in terms of helping each other out.

In her late fifties, Amanda worked part time as a surveyor for Lake County. She also moonlighted by cleaning chimneys throughout the winter and spring. Because she had built her cabin, she owned it and the land outright and was living a life she enjoyed.

Even though Jo had been to Amanda's cabin numerous times, she stood outside looking at it, transfixed by the beauty and simplicity of its design. Prior to building the cabin, Amanda had a load of white pines cut into squared timbers and delivered to her land. She then used dovetail joints to fit the logs together. She created a lofted bedroom upstairs with a dormer-style window jutting out from each side of the cabin. The downstairs had two large circular windows that she painted to look like carriage wheels. She placed a couple of antique carriage wheels decoratively on exterior walls to tie the design together in an artful way. Her cordwood outhouse was constructed out of six-inch logs laid atop each other and joined by mortar. The circular logs were placed whole, or cut and placed in a way that brought out their rustic beauty. Amanda's cabin was the smallest of any of the Big Noise cabins Jo had been in, but that didn't stop Amanda from having it stocked full of furniture and local artwork.

Amanda had crafted a kitchen table out of hand-peeled logs and lumber cut and milled on her property. Jo knew from previous stories that Amanda had traded similar pieces of furniture for much of the artwork visible throughout the cabin. Over the kitchen table hung a wagon wheel that had been fashioned to hold a dozen candles. They provided just enough light for a group of six to play poker on a cold winter's night.

Before Amanda would allow them to begin work, she served up coffee and cookies, and the group chatted for a good half an hour. At the conclusion of the pre-work coffee break, Sandy got up and said, "Gotta go to the post office. See you in a couple of hours." Jo opened her mouth to object but remained silent.

"Can't let the township down. They need their mail."

The first order of business was to shovel off the roof so that they could get to the repair. The roof was fairly steep, so Amanda set up some jacks along the edge so that, should anyone take a tumble, there would be something to potentially break her fall. While Amanda had previously used a snow rake on the first few feet of slope, the rest had to be done from ladders. Once they were through pulling snow down off of the roof with the long-armed rake, Ree and Amanda climbed up and shoveled what was left.

The sun was out, making the asphalt shingles safe to walk on. Jo ventured up to take a look. The view from Amanda's roof was spectacular. Her house sat on the highest point for miles, and she could see two lakes and several valleys in the distance.

They pulled off shingles and boards until they had a ten-foot square section open. The cabin was entirely exposed below, and heat was escaping out of the hole. Amanda descended the ladder and handed replacement boards up one at a time. They set up an assembly-line process to measure, cut (using a handsaw because Amanda had only a small amount of solar power available), and nail the boards into place.

Zoey worked quietly, which was unusual for her in a social setting. But she stuck close to Jo, holding boards in place while Jo hammered nails. They spoke little, but each provided the other with whatever help was needed.

After the group had assembled and nailed down all twenty or so boards, Amanda passed up some tarpaper. Once that was secured, they all descended the ladder for a break.

As they were about to sit down, Sandy walked up. "Nice work!"

"Better look at it from up there," Amanda teased. Sandy quickly climbed up to the roof and proved herself to be easily the most confident and agile of any of them. Inside, the small cabin warmed up again, and the group lounged in relative comfort even though the shingling remained to be done.

"What's that big antenna for?" Jo asked.

"It's an amplifier."

"Does it help with TV reception, too?"

Jo looked around for a television and didn't see one. "I don't see a TV." Everyone except Zoey laughed.

Sandy offered an explanation. "Amanda's legendary disdain for television hasn't made it to the Valley, I guess."

Jo still looked confused.

"Well, let's not get her started on a rant. There are no power lines or phone lines along the Hammond grade, so she put that antenna up to help with reception for her cell phone. None of us believe it actually does anything, but she's convinced."

Jo looked around the simple cabin, assimilating all that she knew about Amanda, and wondered just how absurd this antenna thing was. She apparently went to great lengths to build a simple cabin that was very efficient and minimalist, yet she installed a huge antenna that might or might not aid in reception for her cell phone. Jo finally concluded that Amanda must have had a motivating need for that cell phone. She wondered if there wasn't a sweetheart in the picture somewhere. Maybe it was all part of her duty as a firefighter, but Jo wasn't going to ask, and no one else was talking.

Jo looked around the small cabin in an attempt to figure out Amanda's leisure activities in light of the fact that she didn't own a TV. She noticed a little space set up with music and a violin. A trombone hung from the ceiling. The overstuffed chair in which Jo sat held remnant wood shavings, and a carved fish lay unfinished on the coffee table. Several books occupied the same table, and others overfilled a built-in shelving unit.

"Amanda, I know you play the violin, but do you also play the trombone?" Again everyone laughed.

"Why, yes I do, Jo, especially if you are a bear raiding my compost bin."

The shingling took less than an hour, and when it was time to leave, Jo turned to Zoey.

"Mind if I ask Amanda for a tour of her woods? I want to see this area."

Zoey looked at her quizzically, "Is this about Rick?"

"Yeah, I need to do something here."

Zoey nodded. "Is it safe?"

"Totally. Amanda said that she's noticed a car parked down the grade from here, and I want to check it out. This was several weeks ago. I'll take a look around and let Nate know what I see. It will be a beautiful walk. If Amanda agrees to be my tour guide, that is."

Jo knew that if she uncovered something that could lead to finding her former client, she wouldn't be able to let it drop. She would pursue it until the end, whatever that was. She didn't intend for this to affect their getaway vacation, but she also remembered Zoey's statement that "your heartache is my heartache."

"Want me to go with you?"

Jo took a look at Zoey, and knew that she was beat. "No, we can do this. Go home and get some rest."

Amanda and Jo headed out directly from Amanda's land in search of any clues about Rick. Amanda seemed thrilled to be guiding her friend on her beloved acreage.

It took them about twenty minutes to snowshoe to Amanda's property line. Soon they bisected a logging road. "That car—the old Chevy—was parked on the grade about 300 yards from my driveway back that way." Amanda was pointing southeast.

"What do you mean by 'that car'? Were there any others?"

"Not usually at the same time. I've seen a pickup, seemed like it was full of construction materials one time, but it's been there pretty regularly. And a couple of times I saw a white Explorer."

"Any idea what was going on?"

"Nope. I try not to think the worst about folks."

"Sure, but you must have wondered. If it wasn't hunting season, why would anyone park there and just walk in?"

Amanda, taciturn as always, didn't bother replying.

"And you think he went this way?" It was more of a statement than a question. Jo noted that Amanda spoke quite sparingly. She was one of the few people Jo knew who spoke less than she did. But when she had something to say, it was worth listening to.

"Humans usually take the path of least resistance. All animals do, for that matter, unless they are hiding." Amanda nodded to the narrow logging road.

"We don't even know if the person driving any of those vehicles was Rick. If it was him, it's hard to say what he was up to. It's possible he was just hiking." Not even Jo believed this. If he had been hunting, he might have had a rifle or a shotgun with him. In that case, he could have fallen or injured himself.

"You hear many shots near here?"

"All the time, it drives me nuts. Even out of hunting season. Follow me. I want to show you something else."

Jo and Amanda walked for a good ten minutes before they stopped in front of a tree. Jo couldn't figure out what they were looking at. Amanda pointed to the poplar.

"What are we looking at here? I don't see anything."

Amanda pointed up about six feet to a branch in the tree. "See here."

"Is that a cross?"

"They're all over these woods. Hundreds of them."

"Weird." Jo wondered if perhaps they had stumbled across an area used by a cult.

"You don't know who made them?"

Amanda shook her head no.

"Do they all look like this?"

"No, last fall I noticed one that was quite large and lying on the ground. The smaller ones are usually two sticks tied with twine. Sometimes they are fit together with a dado joint, hand cut with a small axe. Whoever made them is seriously obsessed. I think they made them out here. I've seen axe shavings."

"Tracks?"

"I don't know. I've never seen fresh tracks. I noticed the crosses this fall. Haven't been out here much since it snowed. Frankly, I've been a little spooked. You'll talk to your police friends?"

"I'll definitely tell them about this." Jo wanted to reassure Amanda, but in her mind, she didn't think that a bunch of wooden crosses would get much police attention.

"Thanks," Amanda said. "Let me know what you come up with, if you don't mind." Jo nodded.

She resolved to come back again to check further, now that she knew her way in, and she could use the logging road to keep her bearings.

Amanda and Jo explored for another half hour before heading back. They were losing the light, but they had found one more cross, larger than the first one. Amanda gave Jo a ride home after they snowshoed out her long driveway.

Jo was exhausted by the time she got back to the rental cabin. The morning ski, the conflict with Zoey, roof repairs, and then the trek through the woods with Amanda all added up to a tiredness bordering on pain. Maybe she was trying to push herself past her usual limits, putting off being alone with Zoey. She knew that her lover would want to finish the conversation that had been interrupted earlier.

By now Jo had cooled off considerably about their argument. It was only fair that Zoey should decide for herself where she wanted to live. Maybe living with two rambunctious dogs and a clean freak wasn't all that appealing. At this point, Jo felt more like crying than fighting.

Once home, she took her time warming up in front of the fire. Grateful that Zoey had built one, she hung her wet clothes about the cabin to dry out, consciously draping them haphazardly as if to prove that she could live with clutter if she really wanted to. Zoey had prepared broiled tuna steaks in the gas oven, leaving a plate waiting for Jo on its warming shelf.

Silently watching Jo eat from the couch, Zoey asked, "You ready to talk about it yet?"

Jo crossed her arms, preparing herself for whatever Zoey might have to say. Then Zoey surprised her by saying, "You start."

"OK, so I had my hopes up that you would move in with me. I mean, we are doing so well out here." She gestured to the tiny cabin. "We love spending time together. And we're good together, right?"

Zoey smiled and nodded. "Yes, we are, love. I think we're perfect. My only hesitation is your work. I don't know how I'll deal with you being in so much danger all the time. I'm not sure if my idea that we should continue living in separate places helps that at all, though." She got that contemplative look that she often had when she was discussing one of her former clients or a student in need of help.

"Will you just consider it?" Jo said this with her last ounce of energy. She was bone tired.

"OK, Jo. Why don't we take this vacation to think things over and then talk again?"

"All right." Jo felt some relief that they had talked. It didn't feel great to know that Zoey had reservations about her, though. She knew that she would always love her work and need to do her part in it. It was who she was.

Doesn't she realize that she will always come first with me? More than anything, Jo wanted to live with Zoey, and the sooner the better.

Chapter 16

JO SNUCK DOWN THE LADDER again at around 3:30 a.m., hoping that this wasn't going to be all the sleep she would get for the night. She might have to give in to a nap if that happened.

She went through her nightly routine, but this time she filled her bowl with vanilla ice cream, put two fresh logs on the fire, and let them ignite fully before closing the woodstove door and shutting down the damper. By the time she was done feeding the fire, her ice cream was little more than a puddle. Just the way she liked it.

She thought that what had awakened her was her sub-conscious mind working on the problem of where Zoey should live. They had spent more than two days in the tight confines of the cabin. In her mind, it was going wonderfully. Zoey seemed to have enough space to do her work, yet they had plenty of time for each other. They seemed to move in the limited space with no arguments. They didn't fight about who cooked, or about who did the dishes. She chocked this up in part to the fact that they were still falling in love and that things always started out this well.

No, there were no red flags. She trusted Zoey. She believed that she was who she was with no hidden surprises or hidden agendas. Maybe as a therapist, she really did know what was best for them as a couple. They were both equally invested in this. It somehow felt so much more mature than the other relationships of Jo's life. Jo wondered if she wasn't in her first "grown-up relationship." She chuckled a little at that.

"You OK, hon?" came a voice from upstairs.

"Yah, just thinking."

"We can get you some more ice cream if you run out."

Jo looked up, and Zoey was leaning on the rail naked.

"Want some?"

"Do you want company?"

"Only if you want to join me. I don't want to keep you up."

Zoey descended the steps, thankful that Jo had fueled the fire. "Are you dishing?"

"Sure. Chocolate or vanilla?"

"Little of each, please."

As Jo spooned out ice cream, Zoey found her way to the floor space in front of the fire. She had brought the quilt down from the bed and wrapped it around herself. When Jo came to sit beside her, she invited Jo into the blanket with her.

"Thinking about us?" she said and yawned, placing her head on Jo's shoulder.

"I am."

"And you were laughing?"

"I was."

"And you're going to make me pull it out of you?"

"Yup."

Zoey gave Jo a nudge, causing Jo to chuckle.

"OK, OK, don't get rough with me. I was just thinking that we're grown-ups."

"Grown-ups? As in mature?"

"But still fun." She gave Zoey a nudge back for emphasis.

"OK, but let's see if we can't get some more sleep."

They allowed the dogs to clean the ice cream remnants off of their dishes before ascending the ladder to their lofted bedroom again. It seemed like they both had gotten over their little fight.

Jo, however, couldn't quite drift back to sleep. Her mind kept focusing on Rick. What could he have been up to out here? She missed her connection to Nate and his easy access to all of the police databases.

She decided it was time to check in with him in case he'd learned more from the runaway or about Rick's dealer. If she couldn't reach him by cell here, she might have to drive to Amanda's to test out that amplifier.

Chapter 17

JEAN WALKED SLOWLY up to the small stage with her poem grasped just tightly enough to leave an unsightly crease. She didn't know why she kept coming here to read her work. Perhaps it was because it was far enough away from her neighbors that she felt she could safely share all of her inner secrets. Perhaps it was a way for her to relieve some of her guilt.

She felt guilt every second of every waking moment for cheating on Don, but she knew she couldn't stop. She gladly accepted the free cup of coffee for being able to vent to the world some of what she was going through. She told her husband that she drove the twenty miles to Big Noise so that she could spend time with other writers. She straightened out the paper, without looking up, and started to read.

> Gentle lover,
> guide me from this dream.
> Rain kisses and promises
> upon my parched skin.
> Baptize my arid heart.

> He and his Bible
> strive to martyr me.
> So I hide my scars from his scornful lips
> and cast my eyes down from a looming fist.
> Dogma and duty shall guide his hands.

I imagine a fairy tale rescue
from this vengeance and control.
I cannot endure his worship.
Can you save me
from his sins?

He looks through me with zealot's eyes
as I pray
         and pray
                  he cannot imagine you.

Jean felt very strange as she made her way to sit down. She felt how ominous this poem sounded and knew that it was a way for her to tell her truth for a change and to bring her fears to the surface.

Don knows about Frank, and he's going to kill him. He's freaking nuts. He won't kill me, but if he finds out about Frank, it will all be over. Frank is the only thing holding me together.

She pushed her fears aside, giving in to her rising need once more to take the risk. She had to see her lover soon.

Chapter 18

MORNING THREE AT THE CABIN brought a sense of familiarity and home to Jo and Zoey as they let the dogs out to wander freely on the land, and brewed up some French roast coffee. Jo half expected a knock at the door with a request for help with some neighbor's crisis, but the morning was quiet. The sun shone brightly through the windows of the cabin, and Jo was surprised when she looked at the thermometer and saw that it registered minus thirty. Inside, the cabin easily held a comfortable temperature, but the floors felt cold. They had taken to wearing the liners of their Mukluks over wool socks as they padded around inside.

"Do you remember what Sandy and Ree are up to today?" Zoey asked.

"Not a clue. What do you want to do? Do you have more grading or writing to do?"

"No, I'm on break, remember? How about you? Have something in mind?"

"Not really... How about I walk over and see what they're up to. Want to come?"

"Yeah, I'll join you. I've never been out in thirty below before."

They bundled up in all of their warm clothes, capitulated to Cocoa and Java's pleas to bring them along, and began the short walk. With each step, their boots crunched the hard snow. As they made the small bend in the trail that led to the big house, they both stopped and found the other's gloved hand while they took in the ice-covered branches of a huge white spruce.

"Mother Spruce," Jo informed Zoey.

The snow and ice had weighed heavily on her branches, and she seemed to be saddened by the weight. The tree was higher than the cabin, and half as wide. The smoke from Sandy and Ree's chimney trailed high above their green roof and seemed frozen in place as it attempted to climb up and away from the cabin. Zoey ran in place, and the dogs lifted their paws off the cold snow, so Jo nudged Zoey in the direction of the cabin.

"Let's go. It's beautiful, but friggin' cold out here."

"Ya think?"

They sprinted as fast as their boots would carry them the final distance to the cabin.

Sandy and Ree answered their door in long underwear and the liners from their boots. Jo and Zoey laughed when they saw that their new invention was common practice.

"We were thinking about walking over to see you. Care to join us in our minus-thirty ritual?" Sandy asked.

Jo looked at Zoey. "Well now, that all depends on what it is. Does it involve jumping into water naked or anything equally horrifying?" That made everyone laugh.

"No, it's kind of something the township people started doing by accident. We all end up at G's Café, and some of the local writers bring stuff to read. No one really remembers how it started, but it's what we do. Poetry and coffee in the morning. Some of the writing is really bad, but we have some published poets, too, you know, trying out their stuff." She raised her eyebrows, looking for an answer. "The food is always good."

"We're in. Sounds great."

Jo and Zoey left their dogs in the big cabin with Sandy and Ree's dogs, so that they could enjoy each other's company for the day, and piled into Jo's Range Rover. The parking lot at G's was filled with cars, and once inside, they took the last available booth. The floor was yellow pine boards, and all of the walls and ceiling were knotty pine, yellowed with age. Customers drank coffee, or ate eggs, scones, muffins, and pancakes.

A fire crackled in the open fireplace, and cups and saucers clinked throughout the café as a woman approached the small stage built into one corner of the large open room. There was no microphone—only a small elevated stage and a stool. As everyone sat down, Jo said she would join them in a second and made her way toward the back door where she knew there was a pay phone. She placed a call to Nate, and he answered on the second ring.

"Nate, it's Jo."

"Hey, Jo. What's up?"

"I have to be quick here, I'm at a café. I'm calling to tell you I walked the area where I think Rick went missing."

"Find anything?"

"Yeah. In the woods right by where he was last seen... well, there are hundreds of crosses."

"Crosses? As in religious crosses?"

"All over the place."

"What do you make of them?"

"I don't know. A religious fanatic or a cult of some kind. No one has seen any people, only the crosses. Out in the middle of the freaking woods. I don't think Rick is religious."

"I doubt it. From what we've gathered here, he may have been into meth. Guy used to have a good job, and just left it all. Took the quick trip down, you know?" Jo could hear Nate's breathing. She pictured him running his beefy hands through his thinning hair.

"Maybe it was him," she said. "Paranoid as hell and wandering around the woods building crosses." Jo felt a sadness she couldn't share with Nate. "I thought meth labs were a thing of the past after Sudafed went behind the counter."

"No, there are less of them, but Mexico still sells it in bulk to whoever will buy it. We have middlemen smuggling Sudafed in the mail, on ships, you know the drill. We find a hole to plug, and another one opens up somewhere else."

"You think Rick could have those kind of connections?"

"Hard to say. Thanks for checking it out, Jo, but you don't need to use up your vacation on this case. This is a good piece of information, though. I'll buy you a lunch when you get back."

Jo smiled at that. He was always saying he would buy her a lunch, but neither of them had time to get together so that he could follow through on his promises. "I'm going to take you up on that, Nate. I gotta go."

"Wait, Jo. I'm serious. Don't waste your time on this."

"What's the matter, afraid you'll have to share some of that detective pay with me?"

"No."

"The glory, then?"

"That's our usual arrangement, but seriously, be careful, you hear?"

As Jo got back to their table, a writer cleared her throat, and the noise lowered to silence. A sturdy looking woman of about 35 stood tentatively, without looking up from the yellow legal pad she held, and began reading.

I Want Her

I want her
to be rough around the edges
to laugh just a bit too loud
at parties
or to be too smooth
so that your emotions slip off her mirrored surface.

I want her
kisses to be just slightly askew
so that your lips never quite nestle together
like the hummingbird slipping inside a trumpet flower
for a long drink of nectar.

I want her
lovemaking to be too sweet and soft
without the strength to wrestle your passions into a
steamy tangle of blankets and sweat slicked bodies.

I want her
to fall asleep afterwards
and snore just loud enough to keep you wide eyed,
staring into the darkened bedroom, unsatisfied.

But most of all
I want you
To want me
When she wants you.

The crowd stopped eating and heartily clapped, as Jo turned to Sandy, "Do you know her? Is she family?"

Sandy nodded and waved the woman over to their table. "Sherry, I'd like to introduce you to our friends Jo and Zoey." Sherry shot her hand out to formalize the introduction.

"Nice to meet you. Where are you guys from?"

"Duluth and the Valley," Jo piped up. "Hey, great poem."

"Thanks… I just play around, really. It's fun to read stuff here. I mean, like, there's no risk. We all know each other."

Sherry grabbed a chair and joined them at their table as another poet walked up to the stage. This woman was wiry and grey, wearing canvas work pants and an old wool sweater. Sandy elbowed Jo and in a hushed voice said, "That's Trudy. Listen closely. She's intense." The crowd quieted again, and Trudy spoke in a strong voice.

Sushi

The sea tang of you lingers on my fingertips
As does the memory
Of your anemone fingers racing soft
And silken wet across my skin
To dive and curl hermit crablike
Into my waiting shell of
liquid mother of
Pearl

She looked sheepish after a hearty burst of applause and then continued with a second poem.

Snow Blind

Delicate, intricate, particulate
pieces of ice
slip silent
to the trees.

73

Shaping and softening the
separation between Earth and
Sky.
Bright night full
Moon shines white
on white
goading the field mouse into a
Dance toward death
under the watch of
Owl eyes.

As she finished, the crowd clapped and engaged in a low murmur. Sandy nodded at the group and said, "Kind of a downer, huh?"

That brought a laugh at their table and at a neighboring one. Sherry leaned into Sandy a bit. "I was hoping to see you guys here. I have a favor to ask. I actually had to snowshoe here. Any chance you could give me a ride back and jump my car. I gotta go into town and get a new battery. Mine won't hold a charge. Neither of my snowmobiles will start, either." She looked pleedingly at Sandy and Ree, who gave Jo and Zoey a *"What do you guys think?"* look. Jo looked at Zoey, and they all said in unison, "OK with me."

The stage was empty, so they paid the bill, Sherry collected her snowshoes, and they all piled into Jo's Range Rover. Jo felt a certain amount of guilt about owning such a gas guzzler, but she couldn't bear to think about getting rid of her ancient vehicle. She'd begun thinking about buying a plow for it, and then purchasing a smaller vehicle to commute to work in, but she'd done nothing about it as yet. She took some comfort in knowing that her motorcycle, which she rode to work as often as possible in the summer, got 55 miles per gallon. Maybe it made up for some of her gas-guzzling winter ways. She chuckled a bit at the thought that she was daydreaming about riding her motorcycle on a thirty-below day. Zoey gave her a curious look but didn't dare prod her in public.

Sherry's place was about a half mile north on old County Road 42. On the way, they passed a homestead that looked like a junkyard. Rusty machinery and junkers sprouted like unruly underbrush in between the pointed pines.

The humped backs of mud-covered hogs were visible beyond haphazard, broken-down fencing.

"Who lives here?" Jo asked.

"Shantrees. Why, do you need a car?" Sherry teased, but Jo wasn't in a humorous mood.

"I doubt any of those actually run. Tell me about the family."

"Well, you should know them, most of 'em are on probation right now."

"In Two Harbors?"

"I suppose so."

"Not my jurisdiction. What are they into?"

"Stealing whatever they can. Drinking, drugging, making illegitimate babies. In fact, I had a near miss with a youngin' there."

"As in sleeping with?"

"As in almost. I thought better of it. Can you imagine bringing out a sixteen year old from that family? Those brothers would have eaten me for breakfast. Definitely not worth the toaster oven."

"Was her name Katie?"

"That it was. A real cutie, but she could teach you more about devilry than you'd ever want to know. Do you know her?" Sherry looked suspicious for a second.

"Not really. So, do you think the brothers are violent?"

"Most definitely. They get into bar fights all the time. But it's the patriarch who really makes me nervous. He's insane."

Jo pondered this as they made the turn into Sherry's driveway. The trip up the driveway was another hundred yards. Jo was dumbfounded at the lengths these Big Noise residents went to in order to get around in this community. In her world, women called Triple A. She wondered what Zoey thought of the whole process and looked forward to having a conversation about it once they were alone in their cabin.

"Thanks, guys, I really appreciate this," Sherry said. "Can we jump my car first, and then I'll make you some tea or something?"

Jo pulled her jumper cables from the back of the Rover and hooked them up to her car while Sandy held the other end of the cables apart. Once both cars were connected, they waited an eternal minute for Jo's car to give the dead battery car enough juice for a start. Everyone was hopping in place when Sherry's car finally started. She waved everyone inside, saying, "Go in where it's warm, and we'll be right in."

Zoey, Ree, and Sandy bolted into the little cabin without a second thought.

The cabin wasn't the usual log cabin found in the area. It was still rustic, and hand made, but it was primarily built out of cordwood, mortar, and stone. The walls appeared to be a foot thick, and the structure had a sloping shed-style roof made of long, hand-stripped logs. Like most of the other cabins, it was heated by a small woodstove. The main part of the cabin was timber framed, and many of the logs had designs carved into them. One post had a totem pole theme. The furniture was upholstered in well-worn leather, and decorative and colorful blankets draped over the couch and chairs. A tabby cat eyed her new guests out of the corner of her eye while pretending to look out the window.

Jo and Sherry came in from the cold, and Sherry offered to make tea. Sandy spoke for the group and politely declined. Sherry needed to hit the road in search of a new battery.

On the way back, Zoey asked the group if anyone knew the story of the totem pole.

Ree let out a little chuckle. "It has a lot to do with Sherry's ex. He was Anishinabe."

"He?" Jo asked.

"That was before she met her next ex, Hanna."

Eyebrows shot up all around the car, and Ree waited a beat before replying. "Ron even carved a final chapter in that little pole for Sherry about her new relationship with Hanna, as a way of accepting that this was a part of her journey."

"How long did it last with Hanna?" Jo went after the scoop.

"About two months. Sherry got some great writing done in that time, though. Some steamy writing." Eyebrows went up again. "Since that time, she's had a couple of other girlfriends. She writes about it all. It's been really interesting to watch her be so public about it. Good thing Ron didn't feel the need to keep carving—he'd still be going." That brought another round of laughs.

Zoey and Jo dropped Sandy and Ree off at the main cabin before heading back to their own for a quiet afternoon.

They fueled the fire, then removed their many layers of warm outerwear. Zoey found Jo staring at her.

"What?" She knew exactly what was on Jo's mind.

"I can't stand seeing you taking your clothes off without wanting to remove them all. Come here, and I'll warm you up more."

Zoey walked over to Jo and into her arms. They fit together in all the right places. Jo kissed Zoey, eliciting a deep moan.

Jo whispered, "I think we'd be a lot warmer in bed."

They quickly ascended the ladder up into their loft and made quick work of thawing out from the cold.

Jo sighed contentedly, "Now that should be part of our thirty-below ritual."

"I'll make a note of it," Zoey said in a sleepy voice. They both slowly drifted off into a sweet post-sex afternoon nap.

Jo found herself sinking into another realm. She was walking in the woods looking for Rick. She followed a set of animal tracks into a cave.

The cave was cold and dark and smelled of earth. Even though it was dark, she couldn't stop herself from moving into the unknown area. She stopped and listened. She could smell something terrible. Something rotting from within.

She called out, "Hello? Anyone here? Hello?" The sound didn't echo. She felt with her hands, and the rock walls were becoming narrower. A spider crawled on her neck, and she quickly brushed it off. As she walked forward, the space became narrower. The rocks were now inches from her on all sides, and she had to bend over to move on.

She sensed something ahead. Something was pulling her onward. Now she was on all fours. The ground was cold. She reached up ahead with her hands, trying to see what lay ahead. Her hand hit something. Her hands tentatively explored, and she recognized the shape of a foot. It was a foot in a boot attached to a leg. Her heart pounded, and her ears roared.

"Rick!' Rick!" She shook the leg. "Rick, get up. Are you OK?" Soon she realized that something was shaking her. Or rather, someone.

"Jo, wake up. It's a dream. You're having a dream, Jo. It's OK."

Jo slowly opened her eyes to see Zoey's eyes right in front of her.

"You OK, hon?"

"Bad dream."

"I know. Bad dream about Rick. You were shaking me and yelling his name. Can you tell me about it?"

"I found him in a cave."

"Was he alive?"

"I don't think so. It was so cold and dark. I crawled into this totally dark cave because I sensed I needed to."

"Wow. You hate tight spaces."

"I know."

"Let's get up and have some coffee, OK?"

They sipped silently for a while.

"I have to go look for him."

"Now? It's still really cold out."

Jo walked over to the window and looked at the thermometer nailed to the outhouse. "Well, actually it's getting quite a bit warmer. It's nearly ten degrees out. That's a forty-degree swing."

Jo began to paced.

"I need to go ask around more about Rick. I should go back out to Amanda's land again where we found all those crosses. Something was going on out there. I want to bring Cocoa. She knew him. She might be able to pick up his smell."

Zoey pulled her clothes back on. "Jo, I said I wanted to help, so let's do it. We better stop in at Sandy and Ree's and tell them what we're up to in case it takes us longer than we think."

Their next stop was G's. The owner said she thought she knew a guy named Rick that matched the description Jo gave her, but she said Rick met all kinds of folks at the café over coffee. In her opinion, some of them looked a bit drugged out. Skinny and high strung.

"I thought maybe he was dealing drugs in my shop. I watched 'em pretty close, and Rick always walked his company out to their car, so I never called the Sheriff."

"See anyone in here who knew Rick? Hung out with him?"

"Yeah, there was a young gal who grew up near here used to come in with him sometimes. He seemed real protective of her and never brought her with him when he was meeting with guys."

"Was her name Katie?"

"That's right. Katie Shantree. Her family's a rough clan." She seemed to stop herself from saying anything more about the Shantrees.

"Did you recognize any of the men who met with Rick here?"

"There was one guy I knew, Brandon Reese. Lives in a trailer just off the Hammond up on Highway 44. Turn east on 44, it's the first driveway on your left."

"What's Brandon like?"

"Young. Stupid. Lazy. You know the type. Only works when he has to."

"I can't see Rick as a dealer," Jo said as they got back in the Rover. She was thinking out loud to Zoey.

"If his addiction got the better of him, I could see him stealing and selling hot electronics to support his habit. That's common. He just isn't tough enough to break into the drug trade. On the other hand, that might be what happened to him. Shit!" Jo slammed her fist into her steering wheel.

As soon as she did it, she reached over to Zoey. She didn't want Zoey to be afraid. "I'm sorry, hon. I'm just so frustrated. If a rival dealer got wind of it, he could easily have killed Rick to prevent him from stealing his market share. Rick wouldn't have had a clue. He wasn't that sophisticated."

Zoey sat in silence.

"Let's head over to the Hammond. See if we can see anything else in the woods."

"You can navigate it without Amanda?"

"I have a compass, and our tracks should still be there. I think we'll be OK."

Jo and Zoey and the dogs walked to where Amanda had led Jo on their previous walk, and then headed farther north into the woods. After walking over a mile, Jo came to a cross on a tree. "See this cross? They're all over here. Amanda says there are hundreds of them."

"Wow. That takes some kind of compulsion."

"Compulsion?"

"Assuming they were all made by the same person. I'd say the individual was pretty driven. Likely mentally ill."

"Or it could be a cult."

"Cults are pretty rare." Zoey knew this from her psychology research. "Some type of religious group could have made them, though."

Jo reached down and petted Cocoa. "Where's Rick? Can you find Rick.?"

Cocoa looked around, sniffing the air, and then she scampered ahead at a brisk trot. They followed her for about ten minutes before coming to what looked like a destroyed shed in the woods. All around the shed were smasheded TV sets, stereos, and other electronic equipment partially covered in snow.

The violence of the scene sent a chill up Jo's spine. Either the drugs had changed Rick drastically to make him capable of this kind of rage, or someone else had done it vindictively. The fact that Rick was now missing filled Jo with dread.

She reached down and patted Cocoa. "Good Girl."

"This stuff looks stolen to me," she said to Zoey.

"How do you know?"

"Look at the cut wires on the car stereos. No one cuts car stereos out like this unless they're in a hurry. It's also the sheer volume of stuff. Look at it all."

Jo pulled off a few pieces containing serial numbers, and then she rummaged through the remains of the shack looking for any sign of a meth lab. She warned Zoey not to touch anything with her bare hands. Meth production left some nasty byproducts. The only promising things Jo spotted were a propane tank and a few rusty containers.

80

Chapter 19

"WHAT NOW?" Zoey asked.

"Let's head over to see this Brandon guy."

"You think it'll be dangerous?"

"Not sure. We can scope it out first; then decide."

The driveway into Brandon Reese's place was obviously not plowed. Large, icy ruts scarred the driveway. Jo carefully steered her vehicle, navigating the treacherous roadway for a full 350 feet before a decrepit trailer came into view. It stared back at them, dark gray metal with smoke billowing out of a chimney. Its windows were all covered with blankets, and it sported quite a depressing lack of curb appeal. Outside sat a Toyota four-by-four with firewood filling its truck bed.

"What do you think?" Jo didn't want to force Zoey into something she didn't want to do. "You can wait here in the car."

"I'm going with you."

"OK, you stay by the door. Let me get the Rover turned around, though, in case we need to get out of here fast."

Zoey didn't argue.

Jo motioned for Zoey to stay to one side of the door as she knocked. She didn't want either of them to be in the way of a gun blast, should he start shooting and ask questions later. She could hear motion inside the trailer, and then she saw the flutter of a curtain moving aside at the door.

"Who is it?"

"Jo Spence."

"What do you want?"

"I'm looking for Rick Thomas."

"You a cop?"

"No, a friend. We'd like to come in and talk to you."

Brandon opened the door a crack, but when the cold hit him in the face, he opened the door all the way and hurriedly invited them in. Jo and Zoey stepped inside the door.

The trailer was a typical bachelor trailer. Empty beer cans littered every table. An ashtray was overflowing on the coffee table. Dirty dishes filled the sink and the counter.

"Wasn't expecting company." Brandon rubbed the sandy stubble on his face. He was roughly 5 feet, 8 inches tall, with sandy brown hair, longish and unkempt under a baseball cap.

"I'm looking for Rick. Have you seen him lately? He's missing."

"No, haven't seen him in a long time."

"How long?"

"You sure you're not a cop? You kind of have that vibe."

Jo pulled open her jacket and showed him that she wasn't armed.

She was sizing him up after hearing that he was a lazy loser who didn't like to work. She guessed that the assessment was accurate. He didn't seem to have the energy to be anything but a doper let alone a murderer or gangbanger. Still, she would be careful.

"I don't know, maybe a month?"

"Where did you last see him?"

"G's."

"A drug deal?"

Brandon looked instantly pissed. "I don't know about any drugs." His eyes darted around the trailer, lingering a tad longer at the couch.

Jo shifted her weight slightly forward as he reached for her, grabbing her jacket in his fist. "Listen, lady…"

Before he could finish his sentence, Jo had taken his hand, spun it behind his back, and straight-armed him to the floor face down.

"I thought you weren't a cop."

"If I were a cop, you'd be under arrest. I don't give a shit about your drug deals. I'm looking for Rick." She gave his arm a twist until he cried out.

"OK, OK. Rick shared his shit with me. I haven't seen him in over a month. He left me high and dry. I don't know what happened to him. I've been looking for him, too. Let me up."

Jo did a quick pat search and then eased off her grip a bit and slowly allowed Brandon to get up. "You make a move for me again, and I'll break something. Is that clear? Then I'll come back here with my buddy who is a cop, and he'll bring all of his friends, and we'll have another pleasant visit."

"Look, I don't know who the fuck you are, but I'm not stupid."

"Where did Rick get his drugs?"

"I think he cooked 'em."

"Meth?"

He nodded.

"Where?"

"Somewhere off of the Hammond. He had a shack. I really don't know. We always met at G's. He was paranoid, you know. Didn't want anyone to know where he stayed."

"Where are you getting your stuff right now?"

"I don't have any stuff."

"How about I get my buddies here and we turn this place upside down?"

"There's another guy who sells around here."

"Another guy?"

"Look, he's a mean motherfucker. I don't even know his name, and I prefer to keep it that way."

"Rick's competition?"

"Probably."

"Where do you meet him?"

He nodded no and crossed his arms.

Jo tried several more times to squeeze information out of Brandon, but that was all she was going to get. As they slowly made their way down the driveway, Zoey turned to Jo.

"That was impressive…in a bullying sort of way. Where'd you learn that?"

"Probation staff aren't armed. We have to know how to defend ourselves."

"You've done this before?"

"Not often."

Zoey pressed her lips together in a grim line and looked away.

"This other seller sounds pretty nasty. Brandon was scared enough of him to risk a possession charge," Jo said.

"Nasty enough to have hurt Rick?"

"I can't even think about that."

They drove back to G's so that Jo could call Sandy and Ree with their ETA. Then she contacted Nate as well. She explained to him what they had found and read off the serial numbers for him to process.

"I'll get this to our felony crimes unit and see what we come up with."

"The woman who owns the café here thought Rick may have been dealing. Any idea what might be going on here?"

"Well, it's a big area out there, but that gives these guys some protection. They can pretty much do anything they want out in the woods. Who's going to notice? Sounds like a rival gang thing to me. Has Rick ever been involved in a gang?"

"Absolutely not. He went to great lengths to avoid getting sucked into one."

"When was that?"

"Eight years ago. He was a teen then. I helped him stay out of the Gangster Disciples. I had to help him hide out for six months."

"Shit, Jo, I don't know what to think, then. I'll run the numbers you gave me, and we'll see where that leads. Don't mess with any of his meth buddies. They're paranoid as hell, Jo. Unpredictable."

Jo didn't tell him about her little wrestling match with Brandon, and instead said, "Thanks, Nate, that's good advice."

"Say, Jo. Thought you'd like to know. Good news about that runaway—she's not on meth. I think she saw up close the damage it can do. She's into marijuana, drinks a lot, and she's tried a bunch of pills, but she's got a chance. I actually think she's a good candidate for Drug Court."

"Great, Nate. We can always hope."

"That's what it's all about," Nate replied.

Chapter 20

THE NEXT MORNING, JO WOKE UP knowing what she had to do. She struggled with how to tell Zoey her plans. She didn't really want to bring her along because of how she'd reacted when Jo had to get physical with Brandon Reese.

Katie Shantree was a lead, and Jo had to follow it. She needed to speak to everyone who had been close to Rick. One of these leads would be the string that, if she pulled on it just right, would make everything else about this whole mystery unravel. She was pacing back and forth in front of the stove.

"What's going on, Jo?"

"I have to go talk to Katie Shantree's family."

"The junkyard place."

"Yup."

"You heard what Sherry said about that place—it's hillbilly-ville. It might be foolish to go charging in there."

"I'm sure I've been in worse places."

"Really?"

"We've had to go into properties where signs are posted all over the place warning that if you proceed, prepare to be shot. I'm still here."

"I'm not amused."

"Me, either. I have to go."

"OK, let's do it."

"No, please, just stay here. I'll bring my phone. I'm going to check in with dispatch to let them know where I am. They'll give me a status call every fifteen minutes. I'll be in and out of there in under fifteen. I'll also have Nate run a 911 check on the house. See how many police calls they've had, and for what."

"You don't want me to go?"

"I feel terrible dragging you all over the place on our vacation. It's a fifteen-minute visit. I'll be back in a half hour, tops."

"If you don't come back in half an hour, I'm getting Sandy and Ree, and we're coming after you."

"Make it 45 minutes then, I don't want to call out the cavalry if I'm having a good interview."

Defeated, Zoey said, "OK."

Jo drove out to Highway 41 and pulled over at the crest of a hill before calling Nate and dispatch. After reviewing the CAD 911 report, Nate did his best to dissuade her from going to the house. There were calls for domestic disputes, loud party calls, missing pet calls in the neighborhood, and several theft investigations.

Almost everyone in the house had been convicted of multiple DWIs. That surprised Nate. DWIs in Big Noise were almost unheard of. Nate explained to Jo about the "no crash, don't tell" policy in effect in the area because the only police coverage would be from the Sheriff's Department. Drivers could weave all over the place, and they wouldn't likely be stopped by law enforcement. St. Louis County is geographically larger than some states, and Big Noise is out there. When Nate realized that the DWIs had occurred in Two Harbors, Superior, and Duluth, that made more sense to him. Which only meant that this bunch went out of its way to get into trouble.

Jo thanked him for the intel., shrugged off his advice, and turned into the driveway that led to the house. As she pulled in, she passed old trucks and cars in various stages of disrepair, a rusty bathtub and toilet, and several other household items. The house was a traditional two-story farmhouse with a crooked front porch and dilapidated siding. It looked like it had been painted white once, but now it looked gray.

Off to the right was a makeshift dump. To the left stood a barn and several rusty metal sheds. The filthy slop of the pigpens became more evident as she passed fenced areas leading up to the house. She quickly shut the outdoor air vents on the Rover, but not quicly enough. At least the driveway was plowed, and several cars that appeared to be working were parked along the drive next to the house.

As she drove up, a Rottweiler lunged from the porch at her car, stopping only when the chain he was on jerked him up short.

Shit! Now what am I going to do. A light went on, and the door opened a crack, so she got out of the car and raised her hand in greeting. A large man opened the door fully, but he didn't wave back.

"Sir, can I speak to you about Katie?"

"What's it about?"

"I'm looking for Rick. He's missing."

"Rick's not here."

"Would you secure your dog so I can talk to you?"

"You police?"

"No, I'm a friend of Rick's. I'm trying to find him."

The man put his dog inside the house and walked up to her. He was a good 300 pounds and had on bib overalls with no shirt. Apparently, the cold didn't bother him.

In an attempt to set a friendly tone, Jo stuck out her hand as he approached. "Jo Spence," she said. She didn't want to touch him, but she knew that she had to establish rapport if she expected to get anything out of him.

He returned her handshake. "Walt."

"Nice to meet you, Walt. Do you know Rick?"

He nodded his head. "Sure do. He was seeing my Katie. Way too old for her, if you ask me. I think he got her into drugs."

"What kind of drugs?"

"Shit, I don't know, drugs is all. She wasn't right sometimes when she did come home. Lost a lot of weight. Stayed out for days at a time. No, I don't miss the little fucker. He hasn't been around here in a while."

"How long?"

"Three weeks, maybe a month."

"Did they break up?"

"I didn't ask."

"Did she say anything about him being missing?"

"No, but when I get a hold of her, she's going to have a lot of explaining to do."

Jo figured that Nate hadn't yet notified him that Katie was in detention. Jo wasn't about to let that cat out of the bag. She assumed that it had something to do with abuse she'd suffered at the hands of her father. They would need to investigate that before notifying the alleged perpetrator of her location. "She's missing, too?"

"Haven't seen her in a couple of weeks. I'm thinking she took off with him. Sounds like they went missing around the same time."

"Look, I can appreciate you wanting to have her come home. Maybe we can help each other out here. I care about Rick. I need to find out what happened to him. I can easily work Katie into my search."

Walt grunted.

"Did any of your sons know Rick?"

"Don't know."

"Can we go inside and talk a bit?"

He rubbed his chin. His bare arms and chest were starting to look red from the cold.

"OK, you can come in and talk to my boys, but I want to be there."

The dog growled at Jo as she entered the house, but Walt raised his hand at the dog, and he cowered and sank to the floor. Inside, the old wallpaper in the large living room was stained from roof leaks. Five beat-up couches circled a big-screen TV and the woodstove. Jo counted four semi-grown kids and what appeared to be Mrs. Shantree lying on a couch of her own. No one bothered to get up as Jo entered, and no introductions were made.

Jo followed Walt as he led her into the kitchen. Dirty dishes covered every counter, and ashtrays littered the table. Walt sat down at the table, lit a cigarette, motioned for her to sit across from him, and hollered, "Boys." When no one responded, he banged his fist on the table. "God damn it, get in here. Now!" Four boys slouched into the kitchen entryway. "This woman wants to talk to you about Rick."

Walt got up and poured himself a shot of straight whiskey. He sat down and sipped it, prepared to supervise the whole interaction.

"I'm Jo Spence, a friend of Rick's." Jo waited a beat, and no one said anything. "Have you seen him recently?" All she got in response were shrugs.

"Was he into anything illegal?"

"Look, lady, all we know is what we hear. The guy was into selling hot electronics. He was also a meth addict. Nothing big time." The young man who answered looked barely awake.

"What's your name?"

"Josh."

"Thanks, Josh. Anything will help me. I need to find him."

"Why do you care?"

"I've mentored him over the years. Tried to help him straighten out his life."

One of the young men coughed and said, "Nice work." The rest of them laughed. It took all Jo had not to lunge at him. She was outnumbered, though, and it wouldn't help anything.

She could feel the young men leering, and she was the object of their stares. Her skin started to crawl, but she had to keep trying to get something that might help.

"I found handmade crosses all over the woods where he went missing. Do you know who might have made them?"

Walt immediately sneered, "We're not religious," and took another sip of whiskey.

Turning back to Josh, Jo asked, "Do you know who's the top dealer in this area?"

Again, Walt answered for everyone, "We don't have anything to do with drugs in this house. My oldest son Chip died dealing drugs. First he got shot and lost his sight in one eye. Didn't learn his lesson. Then he got himself killed. Learned his lesson then."

Josh gave a smirk and crossed his arms. She got the feeling that he was dealing drugs right under his dad's nose. She noticed a bulge in his front pocket. It looked like a wad of bills to her.

Jo left her cell phone number with them in case they thought of anything else. Walt walked her out to the car. "I don't want Rick coming around here again."

Jo nodded. "I hear you. He's way too old for her, and I'm sorry he introduced her to drugs." Jo didn't really believe this, but she had to keep the lines of communication open in case she needed to work with this slob in the future.

"If he comes around here again, I won't be hospitable." He hefted his belly up a bit. "That little fucker shows his face, and he may not walk out of here."

"If I find him, I give you my word that I'll tell him he isn't welcome here. You know kids, though, sometimes if you forbid something, they want it all the more."

"Not in my world." He cracked his knuckles and spat for emphasis.

Jo understood that he dealt with most problems through violence. She drove out to the road, called dispatch, and cancelled her status check. She made it home within 45 minutes, and Zoey greeted her at the door, relief written all over her.

"How'd it go?"

"I didn't get much. The boys at that house are pigs. The old man is a bully, and he doesn't like Rick one bit. Doesn't want him around his daughter."

Jo sat down at the table and put her head in her hands. Zoey came up behind her and massaged her shoulders.

"That place is like something out of *Deliverance*. We're talking north country hillbillies. Walt is violent as hell. Thinks he's in control of his household, and his sons are dealing right under his nose."

"Do you think he hurt Rick?"

"He's capable of it. He still wants a piece of him, though. I did find out that they're not religious, so the cross thing doesn't fit. But I don't have a clue about what happened to Rick. I've still got nothing."

Chapter 21

JEAN WAS FULL OF ANTICIPATION as she drove into the long driveway to Frank's cabin. Every time she pulled up to the cabin, she was overtaken by how much she loved this man. *Could it really only be a year that we've been seeing each other? My feelings for Frank are so much more than for Don, and I've been married to him for fifteen years.*

She reminded herself that it wasn't really a fair comparison. Don had changed a lot. He wasn't the same man she had fallen in love with. He'd become more and more unstable.

Because Jean and Frank both lived in Two Harbors, they had to meet elsewhere. Frank had built this cabin as their meeting place. She remembered the last conversation they had had about her possibly leaving Don: "I'd leave him if I could. You have to know that. He'll kill you if he finds out. I'm worried he already knows something's up. Please, please, let me figure this out."

When she saw Frank's old Silverado truck, she felt a wave of relief rush over her. She quickly parked her Explorer and ran up to his cabin. It was still cold out, and she felt the warmth of his woodstove as she entered the cabin. After Frank had built the simple pine structure, she had added her own "womanly touch" by decorating it with colored rugs and throws. The smell of coffee as well as Frank's aftershave permeated the small cabin.

Their stolen moments had been scarce lately because of her sinking feeling that Don knew about them. She took a moment to look out the window to make sure she hadn't been followed before walking into Frank's embrace. Breathing in his musky scent, she held him for a minute without speaking. When she did look up into his warm brown eyes, he cradled her tiny face in both of his hands and kissed her lightly at first.

She murmured, "I missed you so much," and kissed him back with all of the longing she had saved up. He led her directly into the only bedroom, where they greedily consumed each other in their lovemaking.

"I want more of this. More of us." Frank looked pained. He tried to remember all of the practiced conversations he had had in his mind and even in front of his mirror at home before beginning. He visualized her saying yes to his request.

"Jean, let's go away together. We can start a whole new life. I've saved some money, and I know I can make a home for us if we could just leave this place behind."

Her heart broke a little to see him longing like this. "I know that's what you'd like, sweetie. I would, too, except I'm too afraid. I think he knows about you. I'm afraid for you." She looked closely at him for a response.

"Me, like as in me specifically?" he pointed his index finger toward his chest. She could see the fear in him.

"No, I don't think he know it's you, but I think he knows I've been unfaithful. It's making him worse. He's more controlling. It's scaring me more than ever before."

"Let's go, then. I can get a job in Texas. Let's run away together. Let's start a life. Our life. Our real life. I promise you, I'll never stop loving you." His earnestness touched her heart deeply, and she had to admit to herself that she had been pondering the same thing. All that was stopping her was the very real knowledge that Don would hunt her down and possibly kill Frank.

"Do you know someone? Do you have a lead on a job?" She wanted to believe, at least for a moment, that it was all possible.

He smiled broadly as he realized she was seriously considering it. "Yes, my company has a branch down there. I've made some inquiries. I could set it up. I make good money. We could have a life. We could be together." He felt like he was racing to the end of this speech, but he couldn't slow down. He cupped her face in his hands, looking into her eyes.

They heard footsteps, and before they could even get out of bed, Don was standing over them with a rifle pointed right at Frank.

Chapter 22

DON WATCHED AS HIS WIFE, Jean, left the coffeeshop and got into her SUV. Rather than turn right to go toward their home, she turned left. He followed behind in his stolen car. He was glad he'd been successful in stealing the car because he was virtually unrecognizable. Its dark, tinted windows were exactly what he needed to follow her undetected.

Stealing the car had been easy. He didn't understand why so many crooks got caught stealing cars. He had stopped at a convenience store to buy some dry goods for his pantry in the bunker when he noticed that a man had run into the store after leaving his car running. The man asked for directions to the bathroom. Without a thought, Don slid into the car and drove it six blocks away. On his return to get his own car, he went into the store again and bought some gum before driving away. The man was impatiently waiting for the police to arrive so that he could report his car stolen.

Don drove back to where he'd parked the stolen car and jumped behind the wheel. He quickly drove north toward Big Noise and away from the local police. The heater in the little car was pumping out heat, and his confidence grew with each illegal act he committed.

Yes, my fornicating little wife, I'm going to catch you once and for all. You won't be able to lie your way out of this. I'll catch you with him, and then I'll bring you to repent your sins before God. I have been preparing a place for you.

Don felt a sense of strength and purpose and a now-familiar anticipation as he watched her turn her car into the long driveway. He had followed her before, but this time he was ready. Their sacred place was ready, and he would put an end to her sinning. *This was it.* He knew it. He would catch her red-handed. He knew that he was capable of killing in the name of God. He had an erection and felt a little uneasy about how the thrill of being in power was turning him on. He thought about how he and Jean would finally be together again once he righted this wrong. He convinced himself that that was all his erection was about.

He guided the stolen vehicle over to the side of the road and began walking on foot. He didn't know how long the driveway was, but Jean's car was well out of sight as he turned into the driveway. He had brought his rifle and was steeling himself as the cabin came into view. In a matter of minutes, he was standing next to his wife's car. Alongside it stood a dark grey Silverado truck. The temperature was steadily climbing since the low of minus thirty, but it was still cold outside. Don was so angry that he barely felt it. He had sturdy insulated hiking boots, long underwear, a parka, and a hat and gloves. He knew how to prepare for this mission.

He stole quietly up to the cabin, turned the knob, and headed right into the cabin and into the only bedroom. Jean and Frank grasped at the sheet in order to cover their nakedness. The smell of their sex hung in the air.

"Cover your filth, and get up. We're going for a ride." When neither one of them moved, Don took his rifle and shoved it none too gently into Frank's neck. "I said move!"

Frank quickly began picking up and redressing in the clothes he had hastily thrown about the room. Jean didn't move but started pleading with Don, "Don't do this! I won't see him again, I promise!" Her voice was shaking.

"You need to repent. Get dressed!" He hadn't screamed it, only pointed the gun at Frank to get his message across. When she still didn't move, he walked up to Frank and hit him on the side of the head with the back of his hand. This got her shooting out of bed and grabbing Don's hand.

"No, this is my fault. Leave him alone." He raised his hand again, and Jean immediately dressed. Once the two of them were ready, he led them at gunpoint past Jean's Explorer and then to the end of the driveway to the stolen car. He made Frank drive, and he sat in the backseat with Jean beside him. Resting the rifle in his lap, he felt at peace and in control. He directed their turns for about five miles until they turned onto a long driveway off the Hammond Grade.

Chapter 23

Zoey and Jo wandered over to the main cabin. The temperature had climbed up to seventeen degrees, and Zoey told Jo that she didn't think she would ever get used to the temperature swings of this northern region.

"Everything all right?" Sandy asked.

Jo quickly answered, "Perfect, thanks. Hey, we were wondering if we could get a tour of the firehouse and trucks sometime."

"Sure. Only catch is we have some work to do over there. Any chance you could help out?"

Jo and Zoey exchanged a glance that said, *OK, what are we getting roped into?*

"Are we dressed OK?" Jo asked.

"Get the heaviest outdoor clothes you have, and pick us up here in ten."

They bantered about Amanda's antenna for the short ride to the firehouse. Once there, Sandy opened the overhead door with a handheld remote, revealing four red trucks parked side by side.

From the side walls hung hoses, tools, and fire suits. Below the fire suits lay boots. The only thing missing from Jo's childhood memories was the pole the firefighters slid down to get to the trucks.

As they entered, Jo and Zoey inhaled the atmosphere of the place. Hints of smoke and cleaning solution were the easiest to distinguish. The firehouse was heated and a little cooler than normal inside temperatures.

"So, what do you have in store for us?" Jo asked.

"Well, first off we'll give you a two-bit tour of this operation. Then we need to rake the roof. There's a lot of snow up there, and we don't want to risk having it slide off the roof, preventing a quick exit."

Sandy smiled as she saw both of her guests visibly relax. "What did you think we were going to do? Overhaul an engine?"

"Hey, we were ready for anything."

Sandy moved to a lockbox and used a key from her car key ring to open it, revealing several key rings. Taking three out, she tossed one to Ree, and they systematically started all of the vehicles. While the vehicles warmed up, she gave the group a brief tour of the station. She took on a stiff formal tone that neither Zoey nor Jo had heard from her before.

"We can't allow non-firefighters to ride in the truck, so don't even ask." Jo and Zoey both shrugged and proclaimed their innocence with facial gestures.

"The tanker here is basically used for hauling water. The pumper is used to pump water." She began to move away from the truck when Jo stopped her by grabbing her arm.

"Hold on, you're not getting away that easy. Tell us all about it. We want to know everything." Jo looked at Zoey.

"Pumper 101, please," Zoey said.

Sandy replied, "OK," and spread her hands in a gesture that said, *Whatever you want.* She then assumed a stance that indicated she was settling in for a while and began.

"When the pumper is on scene, the operator immediately addresses safety precautions such as access issues, electrical wires, propane tanks, or anything that might pose a threat to our safety or ability to fight the fire. Once everything is secure, we pull hoses off the pumper and start pumping water. The pumper holds twelve hundred gallons of water. While someone is on the nozzle squirting water, others are getting the drop tank ready. A drop tank looks like a big plastic swimming pool and holds maybe fifteen hundred gallons of water." She looked at her guests to see if they were following along, and apparently satisfied they were, she went on.

"Fifteen hundred gallons is also what our tankers carry. The drop tank is set up close enough to the pumper so that a hard-line hose can reach from the drop tank to the pumper. The pumper then sucks the water up from the drop tank to the pumper and out the hoses. So, when the pumper goes through its own twelve hundred gallons, we just pull and turn these knobs."

She pointed rather than pulled and turned. Again, she looked for confusion.

Zoey and Jo nodded enthusiastically.

"We have two tankers, so when one tanker has dumped its load into the drop tank; we drive it to a creek, lake, or a dry hydrant. We use whatever we have close to fill up again while the second tanker moves into position to dump the next load. That way we can pump water through the pumper continuously."

She guided them over to the next truck. "Still up for fire station lessons?"

"Yeah, absolutely, this is cool."

"Our four-by-four brush rig has a 125-gallon water tank. This truck is usually the first rig to leave the garage. Her crew sizes things up and relays the information to the rest of us and to dispatch via radio. They relay details like how big the fire is, where to park our trucks, how close the water source is, etc." She patted the truck with affection, "This rig can squirt water initially to knock a small fire down, but basically it's used to fight wildfires and to handle traffic control. Its flashing lights are good for signaling and guiding a landing rescue chopper, too. It has a long-range radio for communicating with Lukes 1 or Life Flight. We're luckier than most townships because we have so many lakes in the area. Dry hydrants are set up throughout the township that draw water from the bottom of ponds or small lakes, but those are few and far between."

When they walked over to the ambulance, Ree took over. "This ambulance looks old, and it is. We got a grant and updated all of the lifesaving equipment so that we're current. It's a fully functioning ambulance."

Ree jumped into a truck and spoke into the radio. "Big Noise Rescue to dispatch, over. I'm doing a radio check, good afternoon."

"Good afternoon. Dispatch is taking a call currently in your area. Details to follow."

Ree turned to us and smiled, "Looks like you two are getting out of roof raking."

"We can't help?"

"Well, that depends on the call. Want to?"

Jo turned to Zoey, who was nodding yes.

"We're in. I promise we'll stay out of the way."

"You'll do as we tell you to do," Sandy said in a serious tone. "The only possible way for you to help is if there's a lost skier or hiker, and we need a volunteer search team."

"Yes, ma'am," Jo said, only half kidding.

A five long-tone signal came over the radio, followed by, "Attention Big Noise. A cabin owner on Sharp Point Lake reports that a 17-month-old baby has fallen and lost consciousness. A member of the reporting party will meet you at cabin fire number 2807."

"Big Noise Rescue and Engine 4 are responding to the scene."

"Rescue One and Engine 4 responding at 1345," was the reply from dispatch.

"Big Noise portable 12 responding to the scene." Amanda let them know that she would be on her way before them.

Ree looked at Sandy, who pulled Jo and Zoey aside.

"Sorry, guys, this isn't something you can help with. You can either wait here or follow from a safe distance in your car. This may take an hour; it may take five. It all depends."

Jo and Zoey decided to follow at a safe distance. While they understood the gravity of what had happened, they felt compelled to watch their friends respond to this crisis. They followed both the ambulance and a truck for the twenty-minute drive to the lake cabin where the child had fallen. Once at the scene, the ambulance was met by Amanda, who had beaten them there. She was holding a small red flag, pointing them in the direction of the cabin. They slowed and picked her up along the way. Up ahead at a fork in the road, a man holding a similar flag pointed them toward the south gate.

Jo and Zoey stopped and waited in their car for a half hour before the ambulance came back down the shore road. It was followed by a private party car with a toddler in a babyseat, and then followed by the truck. Sandy was driving the truck, and as she drove by, she waved for Jo and Zoey to join the caravan.

At the fork that leads to Two Harbors, the private party turned in toward town. The ambulance and the truck kept going back to the fire hall.

Once they were back, and the trucks were safely stowed in the garage, Sandy said, "Did you see that? We should have had a video of that." Jo and Zoey raised their eyebrows in confusion.

"Right, I mean, how well that was orchestrated. That's exactly how it's supposed to go. Amanda got there first, had people directing the trucks into where we needed to go so that no time was lost. It was like clockwork. A thing of beauty."

"Yeah, we did see that. Really nice. How is the baby?" Although Jo liked the pride her friends took in mounting a seamless rescue, she also needed to know how that child was doing.

"She's most likely going to be fine. She appeared to have a slight concussion, but she's young, and babies are very resilient," Ree offered.

"She was fully responsive and even happy by the time I finished examining her. They're taking her into the hospital for precautionary observation. She's going to be just fine." Ree knew that the child would have to undergo more tests at the hospital before this could be confirmed, and many things could change, but she wanted to reassure her friends.

Just as they had all poured back into the car, the radio came to life again. "Dispatch to Big Noise Rescue."

"Go ahead, dispatch. We're still at the hall."

"A lost hiker is reported on the Hammond line. Reporting party will meet you at fire number 1534 with details." A moment later they heard three responders call in via radio. Sandy requested that all parties meet at the fire number except for Doreen. Sandy would pick Doreen up along the way. Sandy grabbed Doreen's turnout gear (protective fire equipment) and asked Zoey and Jo if they wanted to help on this one.

Chapter 24

Zoey and Jo were more than ready to join the squad. It kind of looked like fun. Heck, the last call had been a cinch. They decided once again to follow at a safe distance in the car. Ree waited for her partner Scott in the ambulance as the rest of the group headed toward the Hammond line. Fifteen minutes later, Sandy picked up Doreen and proceeded to 1534. A tall, wiry man with a short and well-groomed beard approached the vehicle.

Jim Storm introduced himself with a pump handshake. He didn't appear to be shaken by the all-female force squaring off to help him. Jo guessed that the women who staffed this fire department had long since won over the support of the community through hard work and responsive community involvement.

Sandy appeared physically small in this exchange, but she bore the air of chief in her interaction. "OK, Jim, start at the beginning. Who is missing, for how long, and how do we know they're lost?"

He shifted his feet and stood a little taller. "OK. There's a car parked down this road at the end. It's my property, and this is really just a logging road. They didn't get permission to enter my property, so I followed their tracks quite a ways in. Pretty soon, I figured out they appeared to be going in all directions."

"When I bent down to look, I found a place where someone had taken a piss." He shifted uncomfortably and braced himself to go on. "My best assessment is it was a female. Please don't ask me to elaborate." He coughed awkwardly, shifted his feet again, and straightened up. He also adjusted his hat before going on.

"That's what made me notice the writing next to the yellow snow.

Someone had written *HELP*." He stopped for a moment, scratched his chin, and grimaced as though he were looking right into the sun. "I walked back out and dialed 9-1-1."

"Did you tell all of this to dispatch?" Sandy's tone was patient and nonjudgmental.

"No, why? I just figured they were lost."

"How big was the writing? Could you show me?"

He stepped into an area of undisturbed snow and wrote HELP in four-inch block letters. When he was done, he continued squatting and looked up at Sandy.

"Wow, I'm amazed you saw that. It's pretty small. Any other help signs?"

"None that I could see. I did think it was unusual that they weren't using skis or snowshoes."

"Yeah. Thanks, Jim, nice work."

Sandy pulled out her radio. "Big Noise truck one to radio."

"Go ahead, Big Noise one."

"Please dispatch the Sheriff as well to this location."

"Ten-four."

The entire group listened to the call as well as the response and waited as Sandy brought all of the gathering members of the department up to speed. They wouldn't venture into the woods without the Sheriff's involvement.

As Sandy was briefing the crew, Jo found herself watching them and wondering about the dynamics. Scott was the only man in the department. And if memory served her right, he had had a hard time accepting the women at first. Eventually, he learned to respect their abilities and stopped seeing them as "just women." It was clear from Jo's vantage point that he was intently listening and ready to help.

Amanda stood to the right of Scott. Jo found it hard to believe that only two days earlier they had helped her with her roof. It seemed like weeks had passed.

To Amanda's right stood Ree, then Sandy, then Jessie.

Jessie lived on the Hammond on a "compound" that she had built with her partner Bryce. Jessie taught online courses for a college based in Seattle, Washington. Up until recently, she had done this with only a dial-up computer connection. That required patience. Bryce couldn't sign on as a firefighter because she worked full time in Duluth as a speech pathologist in a gradeschool. Fifteen or more years separated them, with Bryce the youngest at 32.

A Sheriff's Department Deputy rolled up in a tan Crown Victoria and ambled over. Sandy motioned for him to meet her away from the crowd. The exchange got a little heated, and Sandy gestured angrily with her hands. He leaned a little closer to her, trying to calm or reassure her. They talked a while longer and then approached the larger group. He was tall and thin to the point of looking geeky. His pants were a little short for him, and as he neared the group, Jo could see his sharp, birdlike features. He presented as the perfect fifty-year-old geek cop with his receding hairline and large glasses.

Deputy Bruns introduced himself and deferred to Sandy to fill everyone in. He struck Jo as very straitlaced. She tried to figure out if she knew him from her work in the Probation Department, but couldn't place him. She suspected he worked out of Virginia, Minnesota. He wore his uniform pants hugged up high on his waist and took his hat off every time he spoke. Sandy brought the group up to speed, Jo suspected in part to lay out the ground rules clearly for Bruns. He listened intently and put his hat back on.

"Searches for lost hunters or hikers are by agreement completed by the Fire Department in cooperation with the County Search and Rescue and the Sheriff's Department as resources dictate. However, given that this could be something more due to the somewhat suspicious 'help' request, the Sheriff's Department will lead an initial investigation. We'll be on hand to support that effort. If no foul play is suspected after the initial investigation, and Search and Rescue hasn't weighed in, we'll resume our normal search procedure. We'll use all safety protocols, including the buddy system and radio checks, since it will be getting dark soon, it's winter, and of course, Big Noise. As we all know from experience here in the Noise, even the deer have guns." That brought a chuckle from the group.

"Deputy Bruns and I will track the party as far as we can, and the search party will follow single file until we've made a determination." She paused and searched faces for any confusion. "Amanda, please brief our volunteer searchers Jo and Zoey while we do the initial tracking." Amanda nodded in agreement.

Deputy Bruns went to his car and retrieved several items of clothing, a flashlight, and a backpack of supplies. He joined Sandy, and they started down the road on foot with snowshoes in hand. Jo ran ahead and asked to speak to Sandy and Bruns in private.

"Deputy Bruns, I've been asked to look into a missing person, Rick Thomas, who was last seen in Big Noise several weeks ago."

"Asked by whom? Who are you?"

"Jo Spence, Probation Supervisor in Duluth. Detective Jerome Nathan asked me to look into it. I used to have Rick on probation."

Bruns didn't hide his concerned look. "What tie does it have to this?"

"I'm not sure, but I thought I should tell you what we found out here." Bruns motioned for her to continue. He looked a bit impatient.

"Someone has placed a bunch of homemade crosses out here in the woods. This is precisely where Thomas went missing." She had Bruns's attention now. "When I nosed around about Rick, folks out here seemed to think he was dealing meth out of G's."

"So, there might be a drug connection?"

"Or gangs and drugs. I also ran into an old shed with stolen electronic equipment. Lots of it. Someone had trashed the whole shed and its contents. That wasn't far from here."

He seemed to ponder this new information. "So, we could be dealing with anything? I'm glad you told me about this."

"We may all be at risk if this isn't just a lost hiker."

"Let's take it as it comes."

Jo returned to Zoey at the back of the group and followed. Everyone in the group had been given headlamps, but no one had turned them on because the sky was still light enough to navigate by.

As they started down the trail, Jo felt a strong pang of intuition that they were in for much more than a hike. She gave Zoey's hand a squeeze and looked at her.

"Are you sure you want to do this? You can bow out and go back to our cabin."

"You're staying no matter what I do?"

"Until I'm sure it has nothing to do with Rick."

"I'll stay." She gave Jo a determined look.

Jo hadn't heard a weather prediction, but since the temperature had risen dramatically within a twenty-four-hour period, a warm front might be moving in, bringing with it a whopper of a winter storm. She pushed aside her concerns, and they continued down the trail.

Chapter 25

ONCE THE GROUP GOT TO where the logging road ended and the abandoned car was parked, Deputy Bruns radioed dispatch with the license plate. Most of the group had radios and listened in. It came back to a Ralph Anderson, D.O.B. 5/12/54, 5' 9" tall, 200 lbs., dark hair. The address on his license was listed as 320 Elm Street, Silver Bay, Minnesota. Bruns asked dispatch to send a squad to that residence and make inquiries.

After the search party left the logging road, everyone put on snowshoes, extra pairs of which Doreen had thoughtfully brought along on a sled. All of the tracks they followed were being obliterated, but that didn't seem to bother anyone.

As Jo glanced at her watch, it read 7:35 p.m. They had all donned their headlights. She wondered how long the initial investigation would take, and what were they going to do about food? They tracked for at least another hour before stopping. The group huddled up, and water was passed around as Bruns and Sandy spoke privately.

The two rejoined the group, drank some water, and then shared their thoughts. They believed they were tracking three people: two males and one female. They hadn't found any more help signs or anything else to suggest that the hikers weren't just lost. The threesome had been traveling in one general direction except in the vicinity of where the help sign had been placed. They speculated that it might be reasonable to believe that the sign was simply vented frustration because the group was lost for a short period of time. Bruns would continue to accompany the searchers, but his initial investigation had not raised suspicion of foul play.

As soon as the group began walking again, the radio crackled to life.

Even though the message was broken, they could all make out the words, "…stolen car…Two Harbors." Everyone stopped in their tracks at that, and Bruns and Sandy left the group briefly for another discussion. When they returned, they signaled everyone onward. Amanda spoke up by yelling, "Request to be heard."

Sandy stopped, faced her, and called the group back together into a circle. It was awkward at first because headlights were shining in their eyes and pointing all over the place. Once people settled in, Amanda said, "We're approaching an area where there are two cabins relatively close together. One is straight ahead and one is a half mile to the north. The one straight ahead belongs to Bart Perkovich. He only uses it during hunting season and sometimes in the spring and fall. The second cabin is on a small lake. It belongs to the Morgans. They come here all times of the year, but it's only accessible on foot, snowmobile, or ATV. There's one more cabin on that lake, but I don't know the owners. They bought it last year."

"How well do you know this area?" Bruns asked as he pointed in the direction they were heading by jutting his chin.

"Quite well, I hike it all the time."

"Can you read trail signs?"

"Human? Easily."

He motioned for her to take the lead with a wave of his hand, and they all followed along behind. Within ten minutes they arrived at the first cabin. Tracks appeared to both enter and leave the front door. It was a stick-built structure that looked to have been a garage kit without the car-sized door. It was lap-sided and had a shingle roof. One small window was visible, and a metal stovepipe protruded from one corner of the roof.

Bruns instructed the group to stay back and keep quiet while he approached the building with his gun strap undone and his hand near the holster. He gave three sharp knocks and announced, "Sheriff… Sheriff." Silence followed. He went through the exercise one more time before entering the building gun first. After three long minutes, he exited the structure, saying, "All clear."

"Well, someone has been in there. The lock was forced, and it looks to me like they were looking for food or guns or who knows what. This cabin

108

was clearly broken into. I'm going to make a call and try to get some help out here on snowmobiles."

He stepped away from the group, forgetting we all had radios, and put in the request. It was now past 10 p.m., and Jo's stomach was growling. After a long and active day, her metabolism was humming right along. Someone must have heard it because after a nudge, she was handed a PowerBar. When she looked around, she saw that everyone was munching on one.

After a little discussion, the group agreed to keep tracking. Sandy relayed the following to the group, "It's going to take snowmobiles a good hour and a half to find this location, and someone is either lost or in need of help." She paused for emphasis. "When hikers become lost and they feel their lives are in danger, it's common for them to break into a cabin to gain shelter. Most will notify the cabin owners and reimburse them for damages."

Amanda led the party to the second cabin, and they watched Bruns go through the exact same routine. The only difference was that the cabin was warm, and embers still glowed in the woodstove. It too had been ransacked.

The group trekked along, following the tracks. Whomever they were following either knew the area or was extremely lucky. As soon as they rounded a small point, they saw smoke coming out the chimney of a third cabin, an old traditional log shelter. The rustic logs appeared to be pine taken right from the land. It was a simple one-story affair with no loft or dormer, one door, and a window on each visible wall. The cabin stood fifty yards from the trail, and a large clearing surrounded it.

The would-be rescuers crowded at the far end of the clearing just off the trail as Bruns went through his routine: three knocks, identifying himself as police. Silence followed. He entered the cabin, and everyone jumped at the sound of gunfire. Sandy yelled out, "Bruns! Bruns, are you all right?" Nothing. The group waited for what seemed like an eternity. Finally the door opened, and three people walked out in a line. The third and tallest appeared to be male, holding a rifle or a shotgun.

Chapter 26

AT THIS POINT, JO TOOK CHARGE. She motioned for the group to back into the relative safety of the woods. The three people walked north toward another unknown destination. Jo turned around, raising her index finger to her lips, signaling everyone to maintain silence. They all nodded wide-eyed. The threesome had probably heard Sandy call out and knew they had company, but they kept walking north.

Jo's elevated heartbeat was pounding in her head, so she took a couple of long breaths and silently celebrated the fact that the threesome had not headed toward them. After waiting for what seemed like an hour, but was really only a minute, Jo motioned for Sandy to follow her and for the rest of the group to stay.

They inched toward the cabin and gently peered in. It was necessary for Jo to open the door more to enter, and the squeak of the hinges sounded deafeningly loud. They cringed and held their breath. Silence followed. Jo entered, and Sandy followed close behind. Bruns was lying on his back. Jo took a quick look around and saw no one else in the cabin. She then put her hand to his mouth and felt a slight breath. She also felt for and found a pulse. She tried her radio with no response. She pulled his radio off his belt, thinking it might have more juice and got a crackly response. She informed dispatch in ten-code that she had an officer down and that it was an emergency. Jo stayed with Bruns and instructed Sandy to go inform the group.

On her way out the door, Sandy turned to Jo. "Who put you in charge?"

"Are you complaining?" Jo felt a little defensive, but tried to appear calm.

"Do you know what you're doing, or are you just being stubborn?"

"I'm trained." Jo thought to herself, *You're not trained for this, what are you talking about?* but she couldn't give up the control. This felt too much like work, and she was used to being in charge.

"Good enough for me, this has clearly moved beyond a search, and he was the only law enforcement officer we had."

"Get your medical person in here…err…. Could you please send in Ree?"

With a dismissive wave, she was out the door. "On it."

Ree quickly took his vitals and rummaged through her bag to find and apply bandaging to his chest wound. She also treated him for shock by finding a pillow to elevate his legs and a blanket to cover him. She hung a saline drip from a bunk and inserted the needle into the top of his hand.

Once Jo was assured that Ree had medical matters under control, she looked around for the Deputy's gun. After a bit of searching, she found that it had slid under and behind a standing coatrack. She set the safety and placed the gun in her jacket pocket.

Probation officers in Minnesota don't carry guns, but Jo had grown up with them. POs in nearly every other state carry weapons, and a longstanding battle existed in Minnesota between the Probation Department and the police, debating whether they should carry. The police think the probation policy regarding guns is nuts. Jo had had too many moments in recent history when she'd agreed with them.

Jo rejoined the group to inform them that she had recovered the Deputy's gun. They all agreed to wait for a rescue team to arrive for Bruns before deciding what to do next. They could hear the faint sound of a chopper in the distance. Jo, though not overly religious, did a silent prayer that he would hang on.

It had begun to snow, and the flakes were heavy and wet. Jo felt another pang of intuition about how big this storm could be. Because she was a native of the region, she knew what could happen with the dramatic temperature changes produced by a cold and warm front dueling it out in winter. Although they were in a clearing deep in the woods, she could hear the wind picking up speed in the trees and gave herself a little hug in a symbolic brace against the oncoming storm and whatever else lay ahead of them.

Zoey came closer to Jo. "You OK?"

Jo shrugged and nodded toward the cabin. "I hope he's going to make it."

"We can leave right now." Zoey brushed snow off of Jo's face affectionately.

"You know I can't. It's too late for that." She looked down at the ground, avoiding Zoey's direct eye contact.

Zoey placed her head down under Jo's so that she had to look at her. "It's OK, Jo. I know this is who you are. You haven't hid this from me. It's all part of the package."

Jo felt a flood of relief and looked back at Zoey. "Thanks."

"I do have a favor to ask, though. I have to pee—can you serve as lookout?" Jo laughed.

"Me, too. Let's take turns."

They quickly walked away from the group and into the woods. Zoey had no experience going in the snow, let alone deep snow, but what choice did she have? Just as she finished, she took a step in order to straighten up and slipped, toppling over with her pants still down. Jo ran over to her and tried her best not to laugh.

Zoey immediately burst out, "So much for being the big outdoor north-woods woman." Jo extended her a hand, knowing better than to make any kind of comment.

Once back in the larger group, Jo went inside to retrieve Bruns's more powerful radio and to check in with Ree. He was conscious. Jo told him that he was one lucky puppy to have a doctor caring for him in the field.

"Yeah, lucky. Right," Bruns said with a wince.

Once Jo knew things were under control in the cabin, she walked back out to Zoey.

"I wonder who the hell that lunatic was and why he has two people at gunpoint."

"You're not thinking about going after him, are you?"

"That chopper will be here soon, and then hopefully some law enforcement on snowmobiles. I wonder if this has anything to do with Rick."

"That was a long time ago." Zoey scrunched up her eyebrows.

"Maybe he's up ahead." Jo pointed her nose in the direction that the threesome had taken.

It was snowing harder, coming down wet and heavy. Jo knew they were all hungry. She had half a mind to raid the cabinets of the cabin instead of asking for another PowerBar.

The sound of the chopper was moving closer, but Jo was concerned it wouldn't find the group because of the heavy snow. She instructed everyone to move out into the clearing, and they waved their arms overhead until the copter hovered directly above. Once they were sure the chopper pilot had them in clear view, they moved so that it could land in the clearing.

The blades created a blizzard as the aircraft descended to the ground, and it felt as though hours rather than seconds passed before the blades slowed.

Zoey and Jo had huddled together for protection and warmth. Jo couldn't help but recognize the seriousness of the situation. The drama of the helicopter landing in a snowstorm in the middle of the remote north woods was not lost on her, or on anyone in the group, for that matter.

When the helicopter-produced blizzard calmed enough for her to look up, she saw that Zoey's entire face was covered in snow, and her eyelashes were iced over. Zoey laughed back at Jo and brushed at her face because she was also snow- and ice- covered.

Two men carrying a stretcher holding medical equipment moved in a fast jog toward the cabin door. Jo and Sandy stepped aside. The men quickly got the update from Ree, lifted the injured man, and were reboarding the chopper when Jo tugged the sleeve of one of them.

"Any chance you can send some law enforcement our way when you get back?"

"Sorry, ma'am, we're going to be grounded after this flight. Only way we got off the ground now was the fact that he's on the force. The winds are way too high for regs. The snow is really coming down in Duluth, more up the shore. It's coming this way, and you know how it is here in the snowbelt. If there's big snow in Duluth, it's massive out here. I doubt you'll be able to get anyone in here. In fact, good luck getting anyone out during this storm. I suggest you hunker down in that nice warm cabin and settle in until it passes."

Jo patted him on the shoulder and gave him a nod. Right before the chopper took off, he threw a bag out. Inside were candy bars and granola bars. Jo gave him the thumbs up, and the big bird took off.

Sandy and Jo conferred away from the group again and devised a plan for the large group to remain at the cabin and stay warm until the storm passed. Sandy, Amanda, and Jo would venture out after the bad guy and his hostages, taking the gun and good radio. Scott would be left in charge of the group and would communicate with them via radio if the signal allowed.

When it came time to go, Zoey pulled Jo aside. "I'm going with you."

"No, you can't. It's safer this way."

"I'm going." She had placed her hands on Jo's upper arms and was looking her in the eyes.

"Ree isn't going. Believe me, this is going to be hard for me, too, but we can't risk both of us." Jo looked over at Sandy, and she and Ree appeared to be having the same conversation.

"We've been through a lot together already, I know, but it's better if some of us stay fresh in case we need you later. It's a good strategy, like the mountain climbers use. You'll be our base camp. We'll get through this, I promise. Stay back, and watch out for each other," Jo gestured toward Ree.

"But do you have to go?"

Jo didn't answer. This was breaking her heart, but not enough to change her mind. Zoey was sullen but held onto Jo.

Chapter 27

SANDY, AMANDA, AND JO FOLLOWED what was left of the tracks. It was still snowing heavily. Although the snow wasn't as wet, the wind had picked up. Jo wondered if they would be able to find their own tracks to guide them on their return. Amanda was reading a compass, and they were relying on her knowledge of the area and her unerring woods sense. Once they had traveled some distance, Amanda stopped and turned toward Jo and Sandy.

"I'm not sure where we're headed. There aren't any more cabins in this direction." She shrugged. "Maybe I missed one somehow, but I doubt it. I've been back here a hundred times."

A little further along, she said, "See this?" Amanda pointed in a tree at a crude cross made out of tree branches. They both nodded.

"I've been seeing these all over the place for months now. It's weird. Like there is some religious fanatic out here doing rituals or something." She said this more for Sandy's benefit than for Jo's. Something about the gravity of the situation made Amanda more talkative than usual.

Jo asked Amanda how close they were to where Rick had most likely gone into the woods.

"Not far, if you come in from the northeast."

"We can't leave those hostages, so I guess we keep following," Jo said.

"This is nuts. He tried to kill a man back there. We're not law enforcement." Sandy was trying to bring some reason into this.

"That could be Rick up there," Jo insisted.

"Jo, he's been missing for too long. It's not likely."

"It's probably connected. I feel it."

Sandy now regretted having that conversation with Jo about following her intuition. "And we can let the police sort it out. This is dangerous."

"I'm going on. You can go back."

Sandy didn't even respond, but started walking again in the direction of the hostages.

Jo tried to radio their intentions. "Big Noise to radio." She only heard crackling in response. The snow and cloud cover must have been impeding the call. Jo decided to go on talking in case someone could hear her. "We're tracking an armed suspect and two hostages in the woods toward an unknown destination. We're traveling north by snowshoe. I can't hear your response but will attempt to provide status checks. We're a party of three, with the rest of the group standing by at the cabin where the shooting occurred."

With much trepidation, they tracked the threesome. Jo hoped that somehow the Sheriff's Department would send snowmobiles from Two Harbors. It was roughly thirty miles. She didn't want to lose sight of the tracks so that eventually she could help direct the rescue operation.

In spite of her earlier outburst, Jo knew that Sandy was equally invested in this rescue. At least as long as it had a chance of succeeding. It was a matter of pride to her that the Big Noise Rescue Squad be known and respected for its response to any crisis or human need.

Amanda was much more hesitant, possibly because she wasn't the one holding a gun. Jo wondered if she regretted having spoken up about her knowledge of the area.

Jo found that she was craving a cup of coffee like nobody's business, and Zoey's plea to go with them was tugging at her heart. She had been on plenty of missions with her juvenile unit at the probation office as well as joint efforts and stings with the police, but she had never really had someone she loved worrying so much about her before. She didn't quite know what to do with this torn feeling.

Sandy seemed to want to make peace, and said to Jo, "Tell me more about your friend Rick. When was he last seen?"

"The teenager who was hanging with him said it has been two or three weeks, but I don't know how reliable her information is."

"Is this still your idea of a vacation?"

"I suppose not."

"Did you tell the authorities about the crosses?"

"Yeah, but it only raised more questions, and there's no proof they're connected to Rick. People often put crosses where they bury pets, or at the scene of accidents. It wasn't enough."

"But Amanda's seen hundreds?"

"At least two hundred. When I called Nate, he said he thought Rick was a meth doper. Possibly dealing. Maybe the crosses were some kind of paranoid delusion."

"Well, that makes some sense. The brain is a strange thing on drugs."

Jo wished her buddy and professional confidante Nate was there to mull it over with her. It might at least keep her mind off their present situation. The snow was blowing so hard that they were in near-blizzard conditions. They could see roughly five feet in front of them, and they appeared to be climbing a gentle hill.

They had their three headlamps, and the other group members had given them two spares. They only had three more granola bars to hold them. After walking for 45 minutes, they gathered for a rest. Amanda was concerned that the tracks they had been following were becoming less and less discernible. She believed they were still on track but wasn't quite sure. The temperature was around 20 degrees, and the wind was strong.

They were passing through a densely forested area, though, which helped to cut the wind quite a bit and allowed Amanda to pick out an occasional track, especially if it was sheltered from the wind by a tree trunk. Hunkering down, they squatted in a huddle.

"So, what do you think?" Jo said to break the silence.

"This is nuts," Amanda said through her scarf.

"Agreed," replied Sandy.

Jo attempted to radio in their status. Probably no one could hear them. If she was getting through, she would surely have heard more than a crackle in response. The radio had been crackling quite a bit, but it was distant radio traffic. She hoped that some remnant of a voice would penetrate the airwaves soon. Once they had rested a bit, she prompted Amanda to share her thoughts more specifically.

"What are your concerns?"

"I'm not sure of the wisdom of this," Amanda shouted through the wind and snow. "My first concern is that we might be lost. These conditions are very tough. I would never go out in this on my own. I've been doing my best to track our direction, but these tracks have gone all over the place."

She had Jo's attention. "We're lost? Can you find your way back?" Jo nodded in the direction they had come from.

"Only if I can follow our tracks. I think this blowing snow is too deep. I'm not sure I'm on any tracks now."

"Shit!" Jo exclaimed before she stopped to think. "What are our options then? Either way, we have problems." Jo looked back and then the other way.

"Well, I'm not ready to say we're really lost yet. I'd like a chance to see if we can pick up the trail in either direction before we decide what we're doing. If we are truly lost, our best strategy is to stay put, find a way to keep warm, and wait for rescue."

Jo looked at Sandy and Amanda. "But you are the rescue team, right?"

"Only part of it."

Jo looked to Sandy. "What's your take?"

"We keep moving in the direction of the hostages, and if we determine we are indeed lost, we should stay put."

"Let's do it?" She met two nods, and they traveled on.

Amanda worked against the snow and wind to pick up signs of the trail. They all struggled with the fear of being lost. Jo had an excellent sense of direction in the woods, and she cursed herself for relying so completely on Amanda. She too had begun to fiercely look for any signs of boot prints.

They walked on for twenty minutes until Jo stopped to bring out the radio. As Jo radioed their status, a shot rang out. It must have been close because sound doesn't carry far at all in a blizzard. They all froze a little more. The radio crackled again. Jo said something reassuring into it, and everyone listened. Jo felt for the pistol in her right-hand pocket and was comforted by its weight.

"That was close," muttered Sandy.

They listened for more sounds.

"This is nuts," Sandy whispered.

"Freaking nuts," Jo found herself replying as she moved in the direction of the shot. She knew from experience that sound can bounce all over the place outside, but she couldn't help herself. She felt a tug at her jacket but ignored it and kept moving. She sensed Amanda and Sandy moving with her. Up ahead, she saw a figure moving toward them but couldn't tell if it was male or female. She lay down flat on the ground and gestured for her companions to follow suit. She removed her glove and drew the gun out of her pocket. The person was walking toward them just off to their right. They lay motionless until the figure was five feet away. Jo whispered, "Stay down."

She sprung up, gun pointed, and in a low voice instructed, "Freeze." The figure immediately put her hands up and sat down. In a sobbing voice, she asked, "Police?"

Jo didn't respond at first because she didn't want to give up any advantage before determining if this was a victim or someone more sinister. "Police or rescue, your choice." The woman began to sob, put her hands down, and crumpled over.

Jo approached her and said, "What's going on out here? Who are you, and where are the others?" Jo had crouched down directly in front of her with gun still pointed. Not waiting for her to answer, Jo asked, "Do you have a weapon?"

"No."

Jo motioned for Sandy to approach and handed her the gun.

"I know her. This is Jean," Sandy said.

Jo didn't seem to hear, or didn't care, and she commanded the woman to stand and place her hands up against a tree. Jo then instructed her to spread her legs and lean into the tree, thereby placing her off balance. The woman still wept but complied, and Jo searched her with her hands. Nothing. Jo called out to Sandy, "Clear." All three of them squatted down in front of her.

Jo repeated, "Who are you, and where are the others?"

"I'm Jean Anderson." She gestured in the direction of the shot and said, "My husband and my lover are out there." She sobbed again. Jo could tell that Jean was small even in her winter wear. She had on a parka and only thin Velcro-closure boots. Definitely not something you would wear into the north woods in winter. Her skin was so pale, it nearly matched the light blond hair escaping from under her knit hat. Her eyes were blue and bloodshot, presumably from squinting into blowing snow and wind.

121

Jo held Jean up by her shoulders and made her look her in the eyes, "How close?"

"I don't know, I think they kept going." Jo relaxed a little.

"Going where?"

"Don is unstable, he's hearing voices."

Jo held up her hand, trying to be patient. "Don is your husband?"

"Yes."

"And the other guy?"

"Frank. He's going to kill Frank."

"Because he's your lover?"

"Yes." She put her head down and sobbed some more.

Nothing about Rick. A Don and a Frank, but no Rick. Jo cursed herself inwardly. She knew she was being insensitive to this woman's plight, but she was disgusted with herself.

She had pushed Sandy to keep going even when her more experienced friend had been warning her that they should turn back.

She'd put Zoey through untold anguish and fear, over what? A damned domestic love triangle.

Jean began taking her boots off.

"Whoa! What are you doing?"

"My feet are cold. I need to rub them."

Jo held Jean's hands still and asked Sandy to come over. "Sandy, can you talk to her and find out what's going on while I see how far ahead they are? I'm not feeling particularly safe here. See if you can warm her feet up a bit."

Sandy nodded, came over, and began taking off Jean's boots while talking softly to her. Jo motioned for Amanda to stay with them as Jo followed Don and Frank, conscious that every step was inching her closer to an armed madman.

Jo couldn't help but wonder why he was heading out into the woods with his wife and her lover. Why not just take care of business at home, wherever that was. Why here?

When it became clear to Jo that the tracks were leading away from them, she turned back. She had eased her fears about their immediate danger. She put the safety back on the gun and returned it to her jacket pocket.

Sandy had removed Jean's boots and socks, and had placed her feet inside her coat and up against her own bare stomach in an attempt to warm them.

"We know each other, don't we?" Sandy looked into Jean's eyes to gauge her response. If the woman was hypothermic, she might not be thinking clearly.

Jean nodded yes. Sandy waited, counting on the uncomfortable silence to prod her on. "I read my stuff at G's. You know, I write. You tried to talk to me." Jean seemed embarrassed to reveal this.

"Don is the person you were writing about?"

"Well, I'm not always writing about Don. Sometimes it's about Frank. In my poetry, I pretend that they are the same person." Sandy nodded in response and turned to make sure it was Jo approaching.

Jo rejoined Sandy, Amanda, and Jean, and updated them on the likelihood that Don and Frank were moving ahead rather than doubling back.

"Her feet were ice cubes because they were totally soaked. They didn't have snowshoes." Sandy continued to warm Jean's feet. "According to Jean here, her husband Don says he has a shack up ahead. More like a bomb shelter. He sounds like some kind of survivalist fanatic. Built a shelter into the earth and is going to survive something we all aren't."

Jo gave Sandy a look that said, *Holy shit, what are we up against?*

Sandy went on to relay what she had gleaned from Jean in Jo's absence. Don had followed her to Frank's cabin, kidnapped them both, and was bringing them to his "bunker." They had been making their way on foot and breaking into cabins for warmth and food along the way. Jean got so tired that she took a gamble and walked away from the group, banking on the hope that Don wouldn't kill her. He did take a shot, but it was probably just to scare her into returning. She kept walking.

Sandy nodded toward Jean, "I know her from G's."

Once Jean's feet were thawed a bit, she pleaded with Jo and Sandy to go after Don and Frank. "He's crazy. He'll kill Frank. Please stop him." She sobbed so hard that her shoulders shook. "I'll go with you. He might listen to me if I have help. He won't kill me. He wants to own me." She looked at Jo with huge, hysterical eyes. Then she made the same plea to Sandy. "This is all my fault. Frank doesn't deserve this. He's really a good, sweet man. Please help him. I'll go back with you. I can talk to Don. He'll take me instead of Frank."

Jo was fighting an internal struggle. She knew what she was up against now, and in some ways, that made things easier. She had dealt with domestic violence many times during her long career. It usually made perpetrators somewhat predictable. She wondered about the hundreds of crosses all over the woods, though, and what that meant about this particular abusive husband.

"Is Don religious?" Jo played her hunch that Don and the crosses were somehow related.

"He thinks God tells him what to do."

Jo shot Sandy another concerned look.

"Does he focus on crosses?"

"Yes! He makes them. He's obsessed."

Jo didn't want to discuss the implications, considering their predicament, but she was certain Sandy was following her thought process.

They devised a plan. As the one most familiar with these woods and equipped with the compass, Amanda would escort Jean back to the last cabin and the larger group. Jo would radio in their location and as many details as possible in hopes that dispatch could hear. Sandy and Jo would push onward to see about Don, his bunker, and the remaining hostage.

They had managed on their snowshoes to close the gap, and Don and Frank's tracks were more visible. Jo and Sandy felt more confident in their ability to follow them now.

But Jo had a sinking feeling about what and whom they were about to encounter. Jo's heart ached as she walked further and further from Zoey. Her relationship with Zoey was the most important thing in her life. She looked at Sandy and sensed that Sandy was struggling with the same thing.

"This is killing me, going into this, knowing that Zoey is back there worried about me. I don't want her here and in danger, either." Jo wasn't afraid, but she was aware that there was still time to turn away from the risk.

"I know what you mean. Ree is always with me on these things."

"These things? You mean you do this all the time?" Jo sounded skeptical.

"Not like this, but the rescues. They can still be scary. You never know what you'll come upon. People are inebriated or hysterical. You just never know." Sandy looked at Jo earnestly, and they stopped to talk it over.

124

"Well, I think we have a pretty good idea about how crazy this guy is," Jo added.

"Zoey and Ree will take care of each other. I'm not worried about them. It's we who need to be careful. This guy is seriously dangerous, for God's sake. And a little crazy—maybe more than a little. That makes him unpredictable. He has to have been planning this for a while if he built a bunker out in the woods," Sandy said.

"I'm with you on that. Let's make getting home to our girls our first priority," Jo added. "But these tracks are pretty fresh. We kind of know where we're going now."

"This is my community. I'm scared shitless, but I feel like I have to do something. Let's just be very careful. Track them until help arrives."

"It's a given, my friend." They locked eyes, and then started back down the trail.

Jo's heart did a tumble in her chest, and she felt an ominous premonition that what lay ahead was something evil and dark. She felt a shiver but told herself that she had dealt with mentally ill clients over the years, and this would be no different.

Chapter 28

ZOEY COULDN'T SLEEP, and neither could Ree. The cabin had warmed to 70 degrees, and the members of the Big Noise Volunteer Fire Department had shed their clothes down to longies. Jackets, hats, scarves, and gators hung from every available surface to dry. They had been talking and trying to rest on and off for the past hour and a half since Jo, Sandy, and Amanda had left.

The snow hadn't let up at all, and visibility was down to less than three feet. Zoey was becoming acutely aware of her knowledge base about blizzards and snowstorms since her migration to Minnesota from New Mexico. While she loved the snow, skiing, and snowshoeing, she found herself awestruck by the power of these storms. She couldn't fully accept that Jo was wandering around in this, trying to track down an armed man holding two people captive at gunpoint. *What did she think she was going to do?*

Ree was no more relaxed than Zoey and turned to her, "So, do you think you can deal with this?"

"What choice do we have?"

"I mean Jo, her job, chasing after monsters. Saving the world?" Ree's eyebrows were raised.

"I don't know. The last time I was with her. This is harder in some ways; I don't even know what's going on. I feel so helpless." Zoey let her hands drop to express her sense of futility. "How do you do it?"

"Sandy doesn't chase monsters for a living…not like this. She…we…put out fires, rescue injured people. We help. Sandy is a bit of a maverick, though. You know, she thinks she's responsible for everyone. Maybe our lovers are cut from the same cloth. I don't know if they can say no when someone is in danger. Maybe they have some kind of a savior complex."

"Something like that. I've been hoping to talk some sense into Jo, but I don't know if she can really change... Damn, I want to go out there and bring her back. I can't stand not knowing what's going on. I can't stop thinking about it."

"Me, either. This is crazy. Why didn't we go with them?"

"Let's go now."

No sooner had they made a pact to go after Jo and Sandy when in the distance they heard the high-pitched sound of snowmobile engines. Everyone in the cabin stood simultaneously and listened. The snowmobiles were moving closer. Ree and Zoey put on their winter wear. By the time they exited the cabin, three snowmobiles pulling sleds behind them arrived. A DNR (Department of Natural Resources) badge was visible on the green jacket of the lead man. He turned off his machine and walked over to them.

"I'm John Tanner. Who can fill me in?"

Tanner was a big man of about 280 pounds. Zoey could tell that his clean-shaven, tanned face was that of a man who spent most of his time outdoors. He was soft-spoken but with an air of authority.

Scott spoke up and did a reasonable job of bringing him up to speed. Tanner pointed to the two machines following behind his and ordered everyone into the sleds for the ride back out. Ree and Zoey stayed put. A brief smile appeared on his face and then disappeared as he said, "What do you two need?"

Zoey shifted her feet a little. "We're going with you to find Jo and Sandy."

He raised his eyebrows and appeared to contemplate the situation. "And why is this a good idea?"

"Because we know them. The snow is going to prevent you from tracking them by snowmobile. We can track them on foot while you follow."

Ree piped up. "Yeah, we can." It sounded a bit ridiculous, but it was worth a try.

He bit his lip, shifted his weight slightly, and rubbed his chin while he looked the two women over. They were all standing eye to eye. "Are you the one who helped Jo take that gangster hit man down?"

Zoey stood a little straighter. "Yes."

128

He turned to Ree. "And you're a volunteer with the Fire Department and an EMT?"

Ree brightened, and a flicker of hope flashed in her eyes. "A doctor, actually. And I have my equipment with me. And yes, I'm trained in rescue."

With a motion of his hand toward the front sled, he added, "I can track them in the snowmobile. How do you think I got here? Let's go, and don't get in my way."

They high-fived and bounded into the sled. Zoey wondered what the heck a girl from New Mexico was doing chasing down a maniac with a gun in a blizzard and let out an involuntary laugh. She couldn't for the life of her figure out why Tanner was bringing them along. She wondered if he was asking himself the same question. Zoey had made up her mind she would follow on foot even if he didn't give them a ride. Perhaps he sensed that and didn't want to be responsible for yet another party wandering out in the storm.

A mile into the journey, the sled abruptly stopped. Tanner had drawn his gun with one hand and held out his other toward Ree and Zoey in an attempt to keep them still. Two figures emerged out of the snow and raised their hands.

Zoey hollered out, "Amanda!" The woman appeared immensely relieved to see them.

The other woman dropped to her knees and sobbed. Ree rushed out with her medical bag to help her. Tanner still had his gun drawn and turned to Zoey, saying, "You obviously know them."

"I know Amanda; I don't know who the other one is."

He squatted and gently asked the other woman her name. Through her tears, she introduced herself as Jean and relayed how she'd ended up walking away from Don and Frank, and her concern for both of them. She piqued Zoey's attention when she mentioned the "bunker" and how Jo and Sandy were planning to go in after Don.

Zoey felt a little dizzy and sat down.

Ree cast a knowing glance her way. When Ree was done assessing Jean, she indicated, "She's cold and dehydrated, but she'll be OK."

She helped Jean slowly get to her feet. "This poor woman has been marching around in knee-deep snow for half a day. It's impressive that she can still stand."

"Let's get her back and then continue." Tanner assumed they would just go along with him. Again Ree and Zoey stood their ground.

"Ladies, don't be absurd. We'll bring her to the cabin, make sure she has a ride out, and be right back at it."

"Go ahead. We'll press on, and you can pick us up on your way back."

He gave an exasperated sigh and ordered them into the sled. "Get in. I told you to stay out of my way. We're wasting time."

Neither of them wanted to chance being left back at the cabin, so they walked down the trail. They heard him mutter, "Women!" before starting up the machine, turning it around, and beginning his journey back to the cabin.

As they walked, Zoey thought of Jo's dogs Cocoa and Java. She had almost begun to think of them as "our" dogs. They were still in the cabin and would be for a long time.

"Ree, I hope our dogs are all right in your cabin for such a long time."

"I'm sure they will be. Hanna lives relatively close to us and will see to that. It's what we do. If she were out longer than us, we would do the same for her. It's all part of the deal."

Zoey was amazed at the love of this little community. Who would have thought that an area as big, spread out, and rural as Big Noise could have so many tight-knit pieces interwoven into it. She smiled and said, "Cool."

The tracks were fairly easy to follow, and the snow had begun to slow. Visibility was back to about ten feet. Zoey reached down and felt one of the tracks in front of her in hopes that it was Jo's. Ree watched her in silence.

When they started again, she sparked up a conversation. "You have it bad, don't you?"

"I have it good," she said with a smile. "I think it has me bad."

Chapter 29

AAAH, MY BUNKER IS JUST as I left it. Safe and secure. No one knows it's here, and now it will serve me well, Don thought to himself as he pushed the captive fornicator inside the stairway leading to his underground haven. The fieldstone had held up well as a foundation. Twelve inches of fieldstone and mortar, and nothing could hurt him. Not that he was afraid. He was feeling particularly strong with his rifle pointed at Frank's back.

Skinny little back, he thought to himself. *What did she see in him, anyway? What could she possibly see in him?*

He'd figure that out later. He was simply there to reclaim what was his. Rightfully his. He was also doing God's work. He knew for certain that this miserable sinner was doing the devil's work.

Don was going to bring justice to the world.

He saw me shoot that Deputy, so he knows what I can do to him. No, he won't be a problem.

Frank stumbled into the fifteen-by-fifteen bunker as Don flipped on the small battery-operated light. As his eyes adjusted, Don watched Frank to be sure he wasn't planning an escape.

No, he's just plain scared. He knows what he's in for. I can't believe the little weasel hasn't pissed himself already. I shouldn't have let Jean escape, but I couldn't shoot her. It's not part of the big plan. They are fornicators, and I'm going to bring them to repent to God. I need Jean to witness his repenting, though. I shouldn't have let her get away.

Don quickly ordered Frank to kneel and then hog-tied him, forcing him to lie on the dog bed in front of the woodstove. He then took his time building a fire and heating up water for coffee. Don went through all of his supplies in the pantry, and then went through them again, arranging everything perfectly. The dry goods were all in good shape. The water was partially frozen, but the container had held. There was enough to last Jean and him several months.

Jean. My Jean. She will come back to me. She will know how much I love her because of what I'm doing. How could she not? She will. She will become the woman I once loved. If she can't, then God will tell me what to do.

He stripped down to his thermal underwear and hung his clothes up on the hooks behind the woodstove and settled in for a cup of coffee.

We can have what we once had. She will again be happy to be a housewife. Eager to please. Eager to keep our home. We will have that again. I need to do this right. Everything will be all right then. Everything.

"Nothing you do will fix it, idiot. You screw everything up, anyway. The end of the world is coming. Nothing you do will keep it safe. Jean doesn't love you. Your only mission is to bring them to repent. You are the chosen one. Only you. You shouldn't have let her go."

"No, that's not true. This bunker is safe. I built it. I am stronger than they are. If I make him repent, it will all be better. I can show God that I know his way. Jean will love me." He was saying this out loud. Speaking to someone in his head. He didn't even realize that he was gesturing with the rifle and swinging it from side to side.

"You don't know. You don't know. You don't know."

A loud blast ripped through the air, sounding like a bomb in the tight space. The bullet pinged off of the stone foundation.

Damn! What have I done? Duck, the bullet is flying all over the place. Get down. Get down.

Don felt the bullet plunge into his forearm. *My right, fucking forearm. How could I have done this?*

He stood there holding his arm in shock and in pain until he could open his eyes. His bone ached, and his whole arm felt like it was on fire. He tried to pull the bullet out, but he couldn't grab onto it with anything, and it hurt too damn much. He wrapped it tightly with an old towel to stop the bleeding. The blood soaked through, so he grabbed a short rope to use as a tourniquet and awkwardly twisted it around his upper arm.

Damn it! I really am screwing this up, like everything. He was right. Dad was right. I will never amount to anything. I'm weak. Stupid! God is just trying to

132

teach me humility. No! I'm the chosen one. I have to do this right.

Don sat down in front of the fire again, then got up and moved the gun into the pantry. He got a bottle of whiskey and took a long pull right out of the bottle, trying to dull the pain. He knew alcohol made his self-doubt and the echoes of his father's voice louder, but what choice did he have? He needed it to be able to work through the pain. As he got up and paced around, he heard a thud on the roof of the building and then another.

Chapter 30

THEY BOTH JUMPED AT THE SOUND of a gunshot. Jo knew they couldn't break their way into the bunker, but they sure as hell could let Don know they were out there. Sandy found a large branch that had fallen from a nearby tree, and Jo scrounged around in the snow looking for a boulder. Finding none, she settled for another large branch hung up against a tree trunk. They threw them as hard as they could toward the bunker roof. After hurling the branches, they dove back into the woods.

Jo had thought about shooting the pistol to create noise, but she didn't want to waste any ammunition. She silently hoped she wouldn't need any.

They waited what seemed like an eternity but heard nothing. After about ten minutes, they devised another plan. Circling the bunker, they realized they were looking at a mostly underground structure. There were no windows, and the door appeared to be made out of thick wood and framed with two-by-sixes. No way could they break in. The earth berming and heavy materials made the bunker virtually bulletproof, which could work to their advantage.

Communicating all of this without words, they retrieved and brought their branches over to the entrance door. Because the door was essentially mounted on a stairwell that led down into the structure much like a cellar door, they could stand on either side of it. They beat the door with their branches. Jo was prepared to draw Bruns's weapon if Don attempted to exit the bunker. A faint sound emanated from the bunker, but they couldn't tell what was going on. They hit the door several more times and heard someone yelling. Because the walls were stone, all they heard was a muffled male voice. Hitting the door several more times produced more muffled shouts.

Frustrated and dejected, they made their way up into the woods while staying in clear view of the door. If this guy was coming out, they wanted to know about it. They took a moment to confer about the next plan of action.

"Well, clearly he isn't coming out," Sandy said.

"What should we do next?"

Sandy shrugged, and they both sat down on a fallen log.

"I thought for sure we could draw him out," she said. "If the guy is that nuts, we must be having some effect."

"Apparently not. Let's hope we didn't make it worse for Frank. God, I hate to think what's going on in there. Isn't there some way we can get in and find out? What haven't we tried?"

Sandy got a little smirk on her face and said, "The roof window." She jerked her head up, energized.

Jo held up her hand to stop her in that thought. "Whoa, slow down. He has a rifle. We would be sitting ducks. Remember our first priority? We have to stay safe here." She looked at Sandy closely. "I'm pretty sure he could shoot at us through the window."

Sandy slumped back down. Jo felt cold and tired. Having to sit still during the majority of the time they had been at the bunker was impacting their ability to stay warm. They heard soft footfalls off to the east and dropped down as far as they could, listening quietly.

Chapter 31

AFTER WALKING FOR about fifteen minutes, they smelled smoke. Zoey eagerly anticipated finding Jo, and she could sense that Ree was equally impatient to find Sandy. They had both picked up the pace, continuing on in silence. The tracks seemed to be going in a circle, so she speculated that the bunker might be smack dab in the middle. They followed the tracks in silence but kept their headlamps on. The snow had begun to slow, so even Zoey could tell that the tracks they were following were new.

After they had walked what she guessed to be a semicircle, they heard a faint "Whoo-aah." It was Jo. This was the special signal they used to find out if someone in the woods was friend or foe. All of their close friends knew it and responded in kind.

Zoey's heart leapt, and she "Whoo-aah'd" back and started running as fast as her snowshoes would take her in the direction of Jo's voice. When she got to her, she hugged her tight. Ree and Sandy hugged each other, too. Once they had reconnected, Zoey updated Sandy and Jo on the status of Tanner and his likely return. Jo told them about the gunshot and their attempts at drawing Don out.

Zoey went numb, trying to absorb what Jo had said. When she gained her composure enough to find her voice, she said, "You did what?"

Jo stood there, fidgeted a little, placed her hands on her hips, and then took them down. Put them back up and forced a weak smile.

Ree repeated the question to Sandy, "You did what?"

Sandy did at least try to defend herself, "There is an innocent man in there with a lunatic. We heard a shot. We had to do something."

"Like run," Zoey blurted.

They agreed to hold tight and wait for Tanner to show up with his snowmobile. They were all hungry and cold and a little peeved at each other. They could afford to be, now that they knew everyone was safe, at least for the moment.

After about ten minutes of waiting, Tanner arrived, and they brought him up to speed. He stubbornly had to make his own assessment about the impenetrability of the bunker and the dangers involved in trying to get at Don and Frank. Tanner was also a little peeved when he heard about Jo and Sandy's attempts to lure Don out. Everyone watched as he made his inspection of the structure and the surrounding area.

Chapter 32

FRANK STRUGGLED to stay upright as Don pushed him down the stairs and into the dark cabin. One dim light clicked on, and Frank blinked at the sudden illumination. The bunker was made of stone and had a roof window, lots of shelving, a kitchen table, and some type of pantry. Don put the gun to Frank's back and nudged him toward a dog bed.

A fucking dog bed. This is how I'm going to die. Please God, don't let me die this way.

Frank's fear increased as Don spoke to himself again as he tied him up. He had been talking to himself off and on all day. Hell, they had been hiking through the snow all fucking day.

Why didn't I recognize it earlier when Don was out of it in the woods? He was walking in circles and muttering to himself. I should have run then. I might not get another chance. If I do, I'm going to take it. Damn, I hope I get another chance.

Frank worried that he had missed his one opportunity. He could barely move his frozen feet and hands, but if he got one more chance, he vowed to run like hell.

The big man pushed Frank down on the dog bed and tied him up. He still had all of his wet clothes on. Don built a fire and made coffee. Frank again heard him muttering to himself about getting her back, arguing about whether or not she still loved him, and resolving to finish what he had started. Frank silently hoped he was not part of what Don intended to finish.

Don was working himself up into a frenzy when he suddenly cowered in the corner and shot the rifle. Frank nearly wet himself, sure that the bullet was meant for him, but he could see from his position on the dog bed that the bullet had ricocheted and hit Don in the arm.

Maybe I have a chance. Maybe God is watching out for me. I promise God, if you let me out of this, I'll do anything. Be a better person, anything. Please God, let him bleed to death.

Frank watched in silent dread as Don pulled things together enough to wrap up his bleeding arm and drink some whiskey. Damn, but Frank really wanted some whiskey himself. He felt he couldn't say anything because he didn't know how Don would react. He didn't have any experience with people who heard voices. He didn't want to make things worse. He knew from talking to Jean that Don could be dangerous. And when Don shot that Deputy at the third cabin, it was obvious what he was capable of.

Frank heard a loud thud on the roof and then several more. This caused Don to shout, get up, and pace in an agitated manner. Frank thought that Don seemed to be hearing the voice again, and then he put the gun in the food storeroom. Frank guessed that Don didn't trust that he wouldn't shoot himself again.

This is good, Frank thought. *If he doesn't have a gun, he can't shoot me.*

Don wandered around the cabin muttering until there were more loud bangs, this time on the door. Frank felt the first glimmer of hope during this whole ordeal.

Thank you, God. I promise, if this is my rescue, I'll be a good person. Please, God. I promise. Please let this be a rescue. Maybe I can see Jean again. We'll get out of this godforsaken place and move to Texas. We deserve to be happy. I love her so much.

Don yelled at the top of his lungs. "No! No! No! This is my time. Mine! You can't come for me now. I built this bunker to keep you out." He then held his arm and crouched over. "It's going to be all right. Plan B."

He walked over to Frank, untied his hands from his feet and retied his hands behind his back. Frank still couldn't feel his hands. He couldn't even tell if they had warmed up.

"Get up! Get up!" Don screamed as he kicked Frank. Frank watched Don go into the food storage room, and when he came out, he had a pistol, which he held to Frank's back. As he walked forward, he couldn't believe he was getting used to the feel of a gun against his back. *A gun held by a freaking madman.*

They walked into the tiny five-by-five pantry, and Don told Frank to wait while he pulled a shelving unit away from the wall, exposing a tunnel.

Don pushed him into the tunnel. It was completely dark, and Frank had to navigate without the use of his hands. He worked his way forward bent over with his hands tied behind his back. He struggled with whether to speak up or not. In his mind, if he spoke up, there was no telling what Don might do. If he did, maybe he could push Don over his edge. He felt way too trapped to try anything. He silently made a plan to wait and make some kind of move when the opportunity presented itself. He wouldn't miss another opportunity. To fight the terror, he pictured himself and Jean living a happy life in Texas.

Frank knew they had reached the end of the tunnel when he ran headfirst into something wooden. An "Oomph!" escaped his mouth. Don quietly ordered him to lie down, and then Don edged forward until his legs straddled Frank's arms. Don opened a hatch of some sort. As soon as the hatch opened, Frank felt the cold outside air rush into the tunnel.

It was still dark out, but the opening was brighter than the tunnel. Don backed up and ordered Frank up. He tried to stand but fell back down flat on his face. He just wanted to lie there. He couldn't get leverage with his hands tied behind his back, and he was so tired. Don grabbed him by the collar and gave a yank, ordering: "Up, idiot." When Frank finally made it upright, Don placed the butt of the gun into the small of his back and pushed him forward again.

Frank stumbled out into the night with Don following. After a few minutes, Don quietly told Frank to stop. Frank watched Don take a moment to listen and look around. It was snowing lightly, and they were standing thirty feet from the bunker on the low side of a hill. There were no sounds, but Frank thought he detected the faint smell of snowmobile exhaust. He felt hopeful that his rescuers were close by. He wondered what would happen right now if he cried out for help.

Why is he holding me? Why hasn't he killed me? Did this mean he wasn't going to, or did it mean he wants to torture me first? He decided not to risk it. Don shoved the pistol in Frank's back, and they walked once again into the woods. Frank felt some comfort in the knowledge that he had escaped the bunker.

Chapter 33

"Hey...over here." Tanner was shouting and waving his flashlight. Zoey, Ree, Sandy, and Jo snowshoed over to the south side of the bunker, where they found Tanner at the bottom of a hill. When they reached him, they could see that he was pointing his flashlight to tracks leading from what appeared to be a couple of rotted out tree trunks. Then he pointed his beam at a hatch door.

"When you first came, did their tracks lead directly here?" Tanner shined the flashlight back at the tracks.

"No, they led to the door. These tracks weren't here before." Jo spoke with confidence. "Right, Sandy?"

"Right."

"We did our own perimeter check, and the only tracks in led to that door." Jo pointed toward the cellar-like door that they had believed was the only entrance to the bunker.

"We better check this out. I need a volunteer to come with me." Tanner looked at the group.

Sandy shuffled and looked at Ree before replying. "I'll do it." Jo looked at Ree, trying to gauge her reaction.

Ree simply said, "I'll join you."

Zoey gave Jo a little squeeze, which Jo took to mean. *Way to go. Way to not be an idiot for once.* What Jo didn't tell her was that she was thinking that one person with a gun should stay back because Don was more likely to be outside than in.

After a long five minutes, the cellar door opened, Tanner yelled, "All clear," and everyone entered the cabin. A single dim bulb lit the space containing a rough kitchen table and two chairs, a woodstove, shelving, and a food pantry.

They stood motionless, sensing the building's raw unpleasantness. Even Tanner, who had already cleared the building for safety, seemed to be stunned, taking in his surroundings. Jo realized that she was holding her breath in an effort to seal herself off from how creepy the place seemed. She could smell a faint coppery smell that she knew from past experience was the smell of blood. She also smelled Don's body odor competing with the dank smell common to basements. This was hardly the cozy retreat in the woods most folks dreamed of building. She sensed her companions were struggling with the same thoughts.

She reached for Zoey and massaged the back of her neck with her hand. "You OK?"

"I will be." Zoey leaned into Jo just slightly, grateful for the support.

"It's warm and dry," Jo said to the group. "And we need that." She looked around and noted that her friends simply nodded without speaking.

Jo felt the need to dispel the gloom and walked over to the pantry in search of food. Everyone else sat at the table. Jo emerged from the pantry with unopened packages and offered them peanut butter on crackers, dried fruit, and bottled water. The rest of the group began to take their wet boots off while Tanner took a look around. They had been out in the wind and cold for most of the evening, and even Jo felt a sense of desperation that she hadn't let herself give into before. She was cold to the bone, tired, and hungry.

"I would leave my boots on if I were you," Tanner said as he walked over to the far side of the bunker. "This nut could come back. There's a lot of blood over here. The shotgun is here, too."

He picked it up and held it up for everyone to see. "I'm guessing you two spooked him with your banging, and he bolted out his escape tunnel. No telling how long he'll be gone." He pointed at the tunnel with his free hand. "Where he's headed now is anyone's guess. We could follow the tracks, but it's snowing again. It's hard to tell how long we would be able to see them."

No one offered any suggestions. Jo noticed that they were all trying to pace themselves with the small meal. While they were creeped out by the bunker and by the fact that a violent man had built it in a paranoid twist of reality, they were all starved.

Tanner unfolded a plot map on the table and stabbed at it with his finger, "This is my best guess at our location." Jo noticed that the map didn't show any structures where he was pointing. The other cabins where they had stopped were clearly marked with tiny building icons. The nearest cabin south of them was roughly three miles away. It too had no road access. "I think this here is the most likely destination," he offered.

"Unless he has another bunker hidden somewhere," Sandy speculated.

"Right. Although that's a possibility, I doubt he could haul enough building materials in for two structures. This is some hike even on a four-wheeler. These stones alone would take an entire summer of hauling." He waved his hand at the cabin walls, "These must be twelve inches thick. I shudder to think about how much water he had to haul just to mortar these joints." He looked genuinely in awe.

"Crazy to me," Jo exclaimed. "Freaking nuts."

Zoey elbowed Jo.

"OK, a schizophrenic," she said in a more professional tone.

"I don't think so. No schizophrenic is this organized."

Jo suddenly realized that having a licensed psychologist on hand could be quite an asset.

"So, can you fill us in on what he is, then? I mean, what are we dealing with?" Jo watched the whole group tune into Zoey.

"I'd say he has a severe personality disorder with paranoid and narcissistic tendencies. He struggles with his own beliefs about the world and how he fits in. His fears are only subconscious. He can't acknowledge them, and he compensates by seeing himself as superior."

"Can you dumb it down a bit for us?" Tanner wanted to understand everything.

"Oh, sorry. I slip into clinical mode. Stop me if I do that again." She looked at the group, then went on, speaking deliberately.

"Narcissism is a deep-seated insecurity that people compensate for by seeing themselves as godlike. They really believe they are superior to everyone, even when they clearly are not. They go to great lengths to protect that image of themselves. Stress will most certainly make him worse."

"What is he capable of?" Jo inquired.

"Well, based on what we've seen here," she gestured toward the foot-thick walls, "he's preparing for a catastrophic event or possibly the end of the world. He's been suffering from this for a long period of time and is, in all likelihood, untreated. I'm just guessing, but he may appear functional a good deal of the time and only begin to show his inward struggles under stress. When he's appearing 'normal' (she made the universal quotation marks with both hands), he may come off as overfocused or obsessed. That's the drive behind all of the time and effort it took to build this structure. Major overkill."

"How violent is he?" Tanner asked what everyone was thinking.

"Well, I haven't done a diagnostic assessment, and I'm going on little information, but based on what he did to the Deputy back there, I'd say he definitely has no compunctions about it. His fears and twisted sense of reality are what trigger him. Most people with mental illness aren't violent. In fact, they're much more likely to be the victims of crime than perpetrators, but there are exceptions." She looked around at the bunker before finishing. "Unfortunately, it's the exceptions that lead to stereotypes."

"Why has he taken Frank hostage?" Tanner kept pressing for more information.

"I assume he got a jolt when he found out his wife was cheating on him. This is probably his answer to that problem. He may be trying to undo the harm done to him, or reclaim what he sees as his. It's impossible to know without having a conversation with him."

Tanner had begun to fidget. Jo knew he wanted to get out there and find Don and Frank. Jo wasn't feeling so motivated herself anymore. It was after 2 a.m., and she was dog tired.

"What's your plan?" Jo asked Tanner.

He shifted in his seat. "I wish I knew where my guys are. They should have been here by now. Either they got lost or they had to bring someone all the way to Duluth for medical help. I have to go after Don and Frank."

"I'd love to help, but I'm bushed. I've been on snowshoes for the past seven hours, and I just can't go any further. I need a rest, and then I'm game." Jo was impressed with her own ability to say no, not usually one of her strong points.

She was very, very tired. Sitting there in front of the fire, she couldn't get up. No one else volunteered until Sandy stirred. "I'm with you. I can go." With a weary smile, Ree chimed in, "I'll join you."

"Sorry, guys," Jo offered. "Come back for us if you need us. We'll be here resting up for the next shift. I'll keep the radio on." Before leaving, Tanner turned to Jo, nodded his head in the direction of the far north wall and said, "That's a crime scene. Minimize your impact."

She nodded back at him. Jo felt a huge stab of guilt as her friends walked up the stairs and out into the cold. Sandy and Ree had been out trudging through this godawful storm every bit as long as they had. Granted, they had signed up for and were trained in searches, but not for this.

Jo struggled to think of a time when she had not been the leader in a crisis. She was always the one out front—using both her physical and emotional will to help others do what needed to be done. She wondered if it was truly physical exhaustion or if her relationship with Zoey was influencing her decision.

Jo was aware of Zoey watching her, but she had to work through this in her own mind. She knew from their previous conversations that her job, and the danger involved in some of what she did, worried Zoey. But Zoey had accepted who she was when they got involved. So far, they had experienced a lot of trauma and intense coping together, but not a lot of just plain daily living. They both needed that. Ironically, that's what this trip was supposed to have been about. Getting away and finding time to be together and do day-to-day, recreational things. She shook her head a little at the irony of where they had ended up.

"You did the right thing," Zoey said.

"Thanks. I really am tired, and I would only get in the way at this point. Let's get some rest."

"Are you sure he isn't coming back?"

"No, but I think it's unlikely."

Jo and Zoey stood together looking around. Jo couldn't imagine herself sleeping in Don's bed. She was too creeped out by him and this place. When she looked over toward the bedroom, Zoey piped up.

"I can't sleep there. It's just too weird."

"Good, me either." Jo looked at the large dog bed next to the woodstove, and they both laughed. Zoey took a blanket from a shelf in the pantry, laid it over the bed, and they both snuggled down on it with their boots and jackets still on. Jo spoke softly to Zoey, "I'm sorry we aren't getting the down time we wanted here. Things won't always be this crazy."

"I'm holding you to that," Zoey said with a gentle elbow.

"I'm counting on it," Jo replied.

Jo made a silent pact to herself to stay awake so that she could alert both of them if Don and Frank returned. She lasted only five minutes before drifting off into a fitful sleep.

As Jo drifted, she dreamed that she was in an aquarium. The aquarium was filled with snow, and she could breathe and swim in the snow. It wasn't cold or hot, and she felt free and at ease. She stopped swimming and rested on a tree trunk.

The snow moved in tiny waves. The waves took on colors and glowed as their colors changed. The colors turned into almost pure white light, and then she realized it was sound. As she listened closely to the sound, she was able to distinguish rhythms similar to the waves. She also saw patterns in the world outside of the aquarium that mirrored the patterns inside.

As soon as she noticed the connection, they all changed into a human voice. The voice was all-knowing and omnipotent. She wondered if it was God. The voice told her that all of the strands connecting everything we know as the world were beginning to unravel. In order to stop the unraveling, she needed to tell everyone about the connections.

She felt the huge weight of this responsibility. If she didn't convince enough people, the world would end. She tried to object but found herself being gently shaken. She tried harder to object and awoke to Zoey shaking her by the arms.

She was saying, "Jo, it's a dream. Jo, it's me, Zoey."

Barely awake, Jo found herself wanting to go back to sleep to argue against being the chosen one. Zoey prompted Jo to tell her about the dream, and then listened carefully as Jo replayed it for her.

"It's very interesting that you had such a vivid dream. You must have absorbed what I was saying about what triggers Don's rage."

"It's interesting—I mean, the human mind and how other people's reality can be so different."

"I love that you have a curious mind." She put her hands on Jo's face and looked into her eyes. "Are you OK? You're not still impacted by the dream?"

"I'm OK. Thanks."

Oddly, Jo felt a sense of home lying in this strange place with her partner. She felt a little overwhelmed with the intensity of her feelings for Zoey. She had never cared for someone so much and was shocked by her fear of something happening to Zoey. She remembered Zoey speaking to her about how difficult it was for her to face Jo being in danger. She found that she had stopped breathing for a short time, but she consciously tried to relax. Sooner than she expected, she settled back into the dog bed and drifted back to sleep.

Chapter 34

They awoke to dull thuds on the bunker door. Jo and Zoey looked at each other.

"God, I wish we could see who that is," Zoey said.

"It has to be Sandy and Ree. Don wouldn't knock on his own door. He'd be a fool to try and come back here."

Jo got up and opened the door a crack. No one was there. She closed the door again, and they agreed that they would go out together to see who had arrived. Jo patted the gun in her zipped pocket before they peered out again. Seeing and hearing no one, they ventured out further when Jo sensed and heard someone in the bunker.

Shit, I forgot about the tunnel.

She turned to look and felt a shove that hurled her toward and into Zoey, who fell into a heap outside. Just as quickly, Jo felt someone grab her from behind and pull her back down the stairs.

The door slammed shut. Such a solid, impenetrable door, and such a final, fatal sound.

When Jo found her balance enough to look up, she was face to face with a large man. A shot of adrenalin surged through her entire body as she realized that this was Don. The abusive, crazy, hostage-taking Don.

She could hear Zoey pounding and screaming.

One thick door separated her from Zoey. She felt Don's eyes watching her think about that door. He took the butt of his gun and hit the hard, unyielding wood, yelling, "Shut up, or I'll kill her."

That silenced Zoey. Don moved close to Jo and shoved the gun up under her chin. "Don't try anything, or you'll both die." She fought the urge to pull away from not only the gun but also his overpowering and disgusting smell.

"Do you understand me?" he growled.

"I understand." Jo had never been held at gunpoint, and she was shocked by how totally paralyzed she felt. One shot, and she would be dead. She wasn't anywhere near ready for dead. She willed herself to breathe.

He slowly moved the gun away from her and pointed it in the direction of the woodstove. Next to it on the dog bed lay a man Jo assumed must be Frank. His face was pale, and he had dark circles under his eyes. He shivered almost uncontrollably and winced as he tried to look up at her. His hands were tied behind his back.

Poor guy, he's been led around like that for hours.

As Don shifted the gun away from her, she resisted the urge to locate the Deputy's gun in her jacket pocket.

Motionless and wary, she assessed her adversary. He looked boringly unexceptional to her. A bit tallish, brown hair, large build. Then she noticed his eyes. They were anything but average. Jo finally knew what the expression crazed eyes meant. Her heart pounded so hard in her chest, she wondered if he could see it.

Frank broke the standoff, "Hey! Can I get these cuffs off? I can't feel my hands." Don aimed his steely stare at her as he reached into his pocket and tossed her a key.

"Take care of him."

She considered whether to obey his order. *Well, I suppose if I'm of use to him, I'll stay alive.*

"I don't have medical training," she said.

"You're a woman. Do what you do."

Jo moved to Frank, who rolled on his side. Deep marks and several cuts from the cuffs scarred his wrists, and his hands looked ice cold.

"Can you feel anything?" Jo asked, alarmed by the desperation she saw in his face.

"No," he said.

After she freed his hands, relief lit up his eyes. "Can you move your fingers?"

"I'm not sure. I've been trying to move them the entire time."

Jo helped him to take off his wet outer clothing and carefully examined him for other injuries before covering him with a blanket.

"Put your hands under your armpits," she told him.

Turning to Don, she said, "He should be seen by a doctor."

"Why? What's wrong with him?"

"I'm not sure about his hands. They look bad. He can't move them."

"Feed him. Get him some water." He pointed at the kitchen area with his gun.

Jo wordlessly searched the pantry to see what her options were. She found a two-burner gas campstove for cooking and several one-gallon water bottles. A five-gallon water container with a spout sat over a plastic tub, which served as a sink. She filled a cup and brought it to Frank.

"Take small sips." She held the cup for him as he took several swallows.

"Fix us something." Don barked the order at her.

Jo found pasta and cans of spaghetti sauce. As she heated the meal, she pondered their fate. *OK, Zoey's just outside the bunker. More help is on the way. Sandy and Ree will be back soon.*

Every molecule of Jo's being wanted to attack Don and overpower him. The thought of the gun in her zipped pocket comforted her, but she hoped that she would have a better chance to reach for it as Don became more used to her presence. She couldn't risk it yet.

I suppose it isn't the first time a hostage has ever had to make dinner for her captor, she thought. *Hell, that was Jean's whole marriage. Probably all abusive marriages.* She was angry at how helpless she felt in this situation. Helpless was a new experience for her. Normally, when things got tough, she dealt with it.

Don ate at the table while Jo fed Frank. He still didn't have full use of his hands, but he had stopped having to warm them under his armpits. He was able to move his fingers a bit, so Jo hoped that they were not permanently damaged.

Jo sat down on the floor next to Frank in an attempt to become invisible to Don. He rocked back and forth and was holding his injured arm.

That injury might give me a tactical advantage at some point, she thought. Suddenly, he banged his good hand on the table.

"Get this mess cleaned up."

It took quite a bit of Jo's composure not to tell him to go fuck himself. If she did get the chance to take him out, it would benefit her to have him see her as meek and scared.

Jo still had her jacket on, and so far that hadn't bothered Don. *Maybe he doesn't believe that a female could be a serious threat to him. Maybe I should shoot him now.*

Washing dishes without getting her sleeves wet would be difficult, but she opted to leave the coat on, banking that his sexist beliefs would keep him from thinking about what she might have in her pockets. As she pushed up her sleeves, she heard a snowmobile pull up outside. Don got up and started pacing.

"No more intereference. This isn't going right," he muttered to himself. "I can do this. I'm not stupid. It's my responsibility. There has to be a witness."

Suddenly Jo knew that she was the witness. *I'm not the target. So maybe I'll get out of here in one piece.* She stole a glance at Frank, who hadn't seemed to hear the comment.

The sun was rising, and she was certain that neither Don nor Frank had slept at all during the night. Don looked and acted ragged. She didn't want to inflame his already agitated state, so she boiled water for dishes and started scrubbing. As she did this, she calmed down and thought logically about her predicament. She knew that Zoey, Sally, Ree, and Tanner were also working to figure this out.

Don paced and alternately arranged things in the pantry before coming out to listen for activity. He spoke to himself in a low, monotonous voice. He comforted himself and dialogued about how, if he could only do what he needed to do, it would be all right. Again, she heard him say, "You are the audience. Bear witness," as he looked at her.

Gingerly, she tugged at the zipper on her jacket pocket a little at a time. She had it partially open but stopped whenever Don came back out of the pantry to check on them.

She made coffee in a percolator pot on top of the gas stove. The lights in the battery-powered lanterns had begun to dim, so she found two gas lanterns and lit them. Soon the rising sun would provide some light through the roof window.

Jo suspected that she had become nearly invisible to Don as she made her way around the cabin doing "womanly" things. She was staying off Don's radar, and she planned to keep it that way. Her only plan at the moment was to get that zipper open all the way. And then she could use the gun.

Chapter 35

THE SNOWMOBILE PULLED UP a half hour after Jo was taken hostage. Zoey found some comfort, during that half hour wait, knowing that Jo was armed. That guy had no idea what he was in for.

Zoey had made her way around to the tunnel opening but couldn't bring herself to attempt an entrance. She couldn't risk the unpredictable impact on Jo inside. Waiting felt like an eternity. Her parka had a hood, but she had to keep her hands in her pockets to keep them warm. Thank goodness she hadn't taken off her boots.

As Tanner and the crew pulled up on a snowmobile and sled, she sprinted over to them. All of her words tumbled out at once, making no sense whatsoever. Sandy held up a hand and motioned for her to slow down. Then she put her hand on Zoey's back and said, "From the beginning. What's going on?"

She told them what had happened.

They all stared at Zoey in shock, and then Tanner spoke up. "Jo's in there?"

She nodded, "With Don and Frank." She nodded again.

"For how long?"

"Half an hour," Zoey blurted, pushed by a sense of urgency. At the same time, she kept thinking, *Why is this taking so long? We have to get her out of there. Let's go!*

After each quick response, she stood there waiting for the next question. She silently counted in her head as they tried to absorb all of the possible scenarios that could unfold in front of them. She stomped her foot, and suddenly they all seemed to focus in on her at the same time.

"We have to do something.," she said in a tone both demanding and pleading.

Ree enveloped her in a hug. "We will. Trust me, we will."

She nodded at Sandy and guided Zoey over to the snowmobile. Zoey realized she was so tense that she could barely sit down. Ree encouraged her to take some deep breaths and talked to her in a soothing voice about how capable Jo was and how they would all figure this out together.

Zoey started to sob. She felt so helpless. Ree held and patted Zoey until her crying jag had spent itself. Sandy and Tanner spent this time conferencing, and by the time Zoey had herself under control, they had agreed on a plan.

It was a little before 7 a.m., and the sun was peeking above the horizon beyond the trees. Tanner and Sandy presented the plan in unison. They stood before the group with their hands on hips, "We wait."

Zoey blinked and stared at them. "We what?" Shock washed over her. She had been waiting an eternity. This couldn't be right.

"We have to do something! Jo's in there."

"Think about it," Sandy offered. "If we storm the doors, we create a situation that we can't control and furthermore that we can't even see. It's too unpredictable. Even if we storm the bunker from both entrances, we have only one weapon—Tanner's. Exploring the tunnel leaves us vulnerable to being shot, or we could end up shooting an innocent hostage. Because our only weapon would have to be in the tunnel, that would leave whoever was at the other entrance basically unarmed. It's a no win. If we wait, we have some element of control." She stood waiting for Zoey to object. Zoey stared blankly back at her.

"Help is on the way. It's light out. The snow has stopped. We're going to have a whole army out here looking for us in a couple of hours."

"A couple of hours is a long time," Zoey insisted, her voice rising. The others stared at her as though expecting her to go berserk again.

Internally, she thought, *Don is unstable. No one can predict how he will react to anything. He's already shot one person. How is he responding to Jo?* Her Jo, the Jo who never knew how to stay away from trouble. "*Fuck!*"

They devised a plan to stake out the two entrances and to communicate movement with two radio clicks. The radios still had power, but for how long, no one knew. Jo had a radio inside with her, and they didn't want to risk unintentionally communicating something vital to Don.

Ree and Zoey watched the tunnel, and Sandy and Tanner watched the main entrance. Once seated on a fallen log, Zoey took a good look at Ree. She had been up all night and had been snowshoeing or out of doors for much of it, but her eyes were bright. "How come you don't look tired?"Zoey asked numbly.

"This is nothing compared to my residency to become a doctor. That was tiring. During residency, I had to make split-second, life-and-death decisions under sleep-deprived conditions. While this is no less important, it's moving a lot slower. The physical exertion helps me to stay alert, too. I really could use a hot shower, though."

"You had to bring that up, didn't you? I thought you sauna'd yourselves clean out here."

"Oh, I still shower every chance I get."

The small talk relaxed Zoey temporarily, and for a second, she almost stopped thinking about what might be going on inside the bunker.

"Thanks for calming me down back there. Did you learn that in medical school?"

"No. They don't teach bedside manner there. Either you have it, or you don't. I was just being another human being. You were so tense I thought you were going to break right in half." She motioned with her hands as though she was breaking a pencil.

"I think if you had come any later, I might have. I'm still not out of the woods." Zoey managed a smile.

"A cracked-up shrink. Isn't that a prerequisite?"

"At least I'm not a jealous one," Zoey said. "You know Jo has a crush on you, don't you?"

"You noticed that? Well, if she's alive, she'll have attractions to people. I don't think you have anything to worry about. Sandy and me, we're lifers."

"Yeah, I think Jo and I are, too, but right now I'm just hoping that it will be a long life."

Chapter 36

Jo settled down in front of the fire with Frank but she couldn't risk talking. She could tell that he was weighing the risks of speaking as well because he kept looking at her expectantly and then looking down.

Don paced and held onto his pistol with his good hand. Jo thought it looked like a 44 magnum revolver. She knew it could hold six powerful bullets. The gun she had tucked away in her coat was a 9 millimeter with what she presumed to be a standard-issue cop clip. Police routinely carry fifteen-round, semiautomatic clips. She thought about conversations she had had or overheard among cops regarding their weapon of choice in any given situation. Now she understood why they engaged in lengthy discussions like the one she was having internally. It really mattered when you needed every advantage.

His 44 magnum is a monster, and can do a lot of damage up close, but it's useless at a distance.

It only holds six bullets and is slow to load and shoot.

My 9 millimeter is more accurate at a distance, lighter, and easier to maneuver. It also holds a lot more bullets.

She realized that she was weighing the pros and cons of pulling her gun and trying to outshoot him. *Am I really thinking about killing him?*

I've had a little training. Probably just enough to make me dangerous.

She knew that people involved in a shooting react in one of three ways. Ideally, everything slows down to what seems like slow motion, and the person's senses become finely tuned. Every smell and motion is distinct. The shooter becomes focused in on the event, and everything else disappears until the shooting is over.

The second way is that everything becomes fuzzy. The person has trouble dealing with reality, and sounds become distorted. They have trouble filtering out any distractions and sometimes freeze or shoot wildly.

The third reaction is either freezing or running, even when the situation calls for action. While she had had the chance to participate in simulated shootings guided by video and sound, it had always seemed like a game to her.

She also knew that, statistically, many trained officers involved in shoots were likely to miss their intended target. *Shit, I'm barely trained at all.*

All kinds of statistics flashed in her mind, but the thing she kept focusing on was that the average trained shooter has a one-in-two chance of hitting a sedentary target. The average trained shooter has a one-in-five chance of hitting a moving target. She didn't know what expertise with guns Don had, but she knew her own proficiency was very low.

He had already proven his skill, though. *How had he managed to get the drop on Deputy Bruns, someone with a lot more experience than I have?*

Another phrase kept cycling through her head. *A weapon in the hands of an untrained person increases the likelihood of his or her death.* The effect that Don's mental illness would have on the situation was unknown.

She shook her head to free herself of this line of thinking. She knew that she had an uncanny ability to talk her way out of situations. When he saw her shake her head, Frank gave her a quizzical and concerned look. She winked reassuringly at him and turned her attention back to Don.

He sat at the table writing, stopping periodically to hold his arm and flex his fingers. Jo saw blood soaking through a makeshift bandage wrapped around his arm. She wanted to wrench his arm until he screamed in pain and then take his gun.

She finally broke the silence that had been working thus far to keep her off of his radar. She needed to get a bead on where he was at.

"Don."

When he looked up, his head jerked and his eyes gained focus. Rejoining present-day reality, Jo guessed. He looked at her in silence for a moment and then replied, "What?"

She hadn't planned what she would say to him, so she was winging it. "Is your full name Donald?"

As she said it, he flinched.

"We've been over this. Don't call me Donald."

We've been over this? Does he think I'm someone else? "Sorry, Don. Can I get you some more coffee?"

"Please." He held up his cup momentarily and then resumed writing. Maybe he assumed that this was the typical role women played. She hoped she could pull it off. She got up to serve him coffee and lingered over his shoulder long enough to glance at what he was writing. She could make out "God," "end," "fuck-up," and "mine." Not wanting to linger too long, she eased away.

She doubted how far she could carry the charade of being a doting woman. What if he wanted affection? The thought of trying to cozy up to him was likely to make her gag, which would surely give her away as an imposter.

Jo decided to clean the propane stove. She reflected back on Zoey's comments about her being just shy of obsessive compulsive and knew that on some level she needed to clean something in order to feel in control over what was happening. She found Brillo pads in the sink cabinet and scrubbed away. The stove would at least offer her some stress relief.

Don seemed to relax a bit as she went after the stove. Frank's eyebrows were raised, and Jo believed he was confused as hell. Jo sent him a look that said, *Once we get out of here, if you tell anyone about this, I'm going to kill you myself.*

Jo noticed that Frank was starting to squirm. She hoped he wasn't thinking about trying something. He could easily set Don off. Jo shook her head "no" toward him. He seemed to settle down and then spoke up, "I need to use the bathroom."

Don got up and took two small steps over to him, pointed the handgun in the direction of a closet-sized bathroom, and said, "Over there."

Jo started thinking about opportunities for escape, or of taking Don down. The two men got to the bathroom, and Don stood in the doorway observing Frank. He didn't seem to be paying any attention to her, but he could be listening. Jo knew from her explorations that all the room contained was a sink with a water jug perched on top and a Porta-Potty.

Jo's gun was still safely tucked inside the now unzipped pocket of her jacket. The main doorway leading up and out was ten feet to the right of the bathroom closet. Don stood between the bathroom opening and the outer door, leaving perhaps seven feet from him to the door. He was too close. Everything was too close.

Jo slipped her hand into her pocket and touched the gun, but Don seemed to sense her watching him and turned toward her again. She looked inside the cooler next to the counter. It was empty, so she pulled it up and cleaned it with bleach. Don escorted Frank back to the dog bed and said, "Sit, you ugly mutt." His rage began to redden his face. "Was it worth it?"

Frank didn't look at him and sat.

"On second thought, get up. I'm going to show you something." He motioned with his gun for Frank to get up. He then pointed it at Jo, "You, too."

As he led them over to the middle of the room, he instructed Jo to move the rug. When she did, a trapdoor became visible. "Open it."

When she pulled open the door, a rush of frigid air hit her. Along with the air came the distinct smell of death. She was looking at what appeared to be a cellar dug deeper under the bunker. *Wow, this guy has been planning this and preparing for a long time.*

"In," he barked.

Frank descended the stairs, abruptly stopped, and backed up into them. Jo felt a shove from behind, and the butt of Don's gun pressed into her back.

"Keep going." When Frank turned to face Jo, he was ashen. His eyes pleaded. She gave him a look that said, *Go, or we're dead.* Thankfully, he kept going. It was darker inside, but Jo could still see the ghastly figure in front of her.

Before them knelt a dead man held up by rope so that he appeared to be posed in prayer. His arms and hands were secured palms together, elevated by thin rope tied to the floor joists of the cabin above. His head hung down so that his face wasn't visible.

Jo slowly approached and crouched down so that she could see the face of this corpse. The look on the dead man's face was anything but serene. His mouth was open as if caught in a horrific scream. Blood had oozed out of his eyes, making the whole scene look oddly religious.

The blood drained from Jo's face, and she saw stars. Instinctively, she reached for a wall to steady herself. It was Rick.

She knew on a deep level that this gross scene would be burned into her memory forever. She knew she should look away, but she was transfixed. Rick's skin had sagged, and his eyes were deep sockets. His hair had fallen out in patches.

She shook her head as if to erase the image from her mind. Then her shock turned to rage.

"What the hell is this?" She turned on Don and wanted to pummel him to death. She couldn't ever remember feeling such fury. The only thing stopping her was his gun.

Don didn't answer her right away but hummed to himself and stared off into the distance.

Chapter 37

THE DAY HE HAD FOUND this sinner came flooding back. God must have been guiding him. He woke up that morning feeling the strong pull of purpose. Bolstered by his destruction of the shack containing the electronics only weeks before, he believed that he was answering a calling from God—that he was the chosen one not only to bring justice to his small corner of the world but also to rid the world of sinners.

He had been walking out in the woods less than an hour from his bunker when he heard someone shooting. He'd placed several crosses in the woods along the way so that he could find his way back to the bunker. It was winter, post-hunting season, so the shooter had to be a poacher or perhaps someone taking target practice. He knew these woods inside and out because he had spent the better part of a year building his retreat and marking the area around it with his crosses. He had spent every waking second he could spare, when he was away from his wife and his work, out in the woods near Big Noise.

In part, he had picked this spot because his wife loved to hang out at G's, the local café. He was certain she had been seeing someone, and this spot allowed him to stay close, so he could keep tabs on her. Jean knew nothing of his secret bunker. She didn't seem to care what he was doing, and she seemed happy each time he said that he was going away from home.

The shooting stopped, and he listened closely, careful to stay quiet himself as he honed in on his target. He could make out the faint banging of metal on metal. He crept in the direction of the noise. When he was close enough to see what was going on, he hid behind a tree. Checking his rifle, he instinctively sniffed the air. The faint smell of what he thought was cat urine wafted toward him. If this is what drug making smelled like, it was a sure sign that the sinners who did it were headed for hell.

He felt elated at this discovery because he could right another wrong. He felt sure that God had guided him to this place today to help this man repent for his sin. As he approached, he could see the man working on something under a makeshift tarp. The gun that he had been shooting was leaning under a tree, and a dead squirrel lay next to it on the snow. Don crept up slowly, careful not to make a sound until he was close to the gun and within ten feet of the sinner. Don had heard that meth labs were volatile, and he thought he could potentially blow them both up if he wasn't careful. He was willing to give his life for his cause, but he would avoid it if possible. He knew God was watching him, guiding him. Maybe this was the little weasel his wife was seeing. He would soon enough find out.

He quickly ran up to and grabbed the gun leaning up against the tree and threw it behind him into the woods. After he did that, he leveled his own rifle at the man.

"What the? Hey, easy…" the man said as he raised his hands. "Who are you?"

Don didn't want to give up any advantage, "Who are you?"

"I'm just a guy…hanging out in the woods. Take it easy."

Don fired off a round into a tree to the right of the man, who visibly jumped and began to sweat.

"Who are you? I won't ask again." Don looked at him with a steely resolve.

"Rick Thomas."

"This your meth lab?" Don pointed with his gun toward the burners and containers.

"I know my rights. I want a lawyer!"

"A lawyer won't help you here, Rick. You're a sinner, and I'm going to make you repent."

Rick felt as if his bowels were going to let loose. He had a sinking feeling that he wished this guy was a cop rather than some religious fanatic. *Holy shit, what am I in for here. I have to get my gun back or find a way to get away from this guy.*

168

Maybe he isn't really dangerous if he's religious. He did take a shot that went right by my head, though.

"What do you want?" Rick said. He was trying not to shake, but he was certain his knees were knocking together. He'd been tweaking on a previous batch of meth for the past several days and hadn't slept.

"You're coming with me, unless you would rather die."

"Where are we going?"

"To your salvation."

Rick's mind was racing, due in part to the meth. He had been getting progressively more paranoid as his use increased over the past year, and this was really straining his ability to stay within reality. He wanted to explode at this crazy man, but somehow he kept his thoughts under control and started walking. He planned to bide his time until he could get away, or overpower this guy. *What the hell will happen to me if my meth wears off?*

They walked for about an hour before coming to a small, nearly hidden structure built into the ground. As they stood in front of a door that led underground, Don instructed him to "Pray for your soul. I know you've been cheating with my wife."

"Your wife? I don't even know you. I don't know your wife." By now Rick was craving a fix like a starving man craves food. "I need my drugs. I can't function without them. You can't do this." He was beginning not to care about the gun, or what happened to him.

Don wanted to hit him, but he also relished the control he had when he held himself back. He had to believe this was about principles rather than power. Doing the work of God was so satisfying. He thought ahead to the place he had set up in his bunker where he prayed and knew that it was the spot where Rick had to pray for his forgiveness. He needed to teach him how to pray properly before they moved inside.

If I just make this right, Jean will stop running from me, and we will be happy again. She will again be the loving wife that she vowed to be. He knew what he had to do. "Get down on your knees and ask for forgiveness. You have sinned in the eyes of the Lord. You have committed adultery."

"I'll do it if I can have my drugs. I have them here. I have a rig." He dug into the big side pocket of his military-style camouflage pants. Don let him and watched in fascination as Rick cut his meth, heated it up in a spoon until it liquefied, tied up his arm so that his vein was visible, drew the liquid up into a syringe, and injected himself.

"God is your witness. This has destroyed you. Kneel before him in humility for your sins."

Rick no longer cared about anything except the sweet ecstasy of getting high. In reality, it wasn't so much a high anymore as it was getting back to being able to function. When he didn't have ready access to meth, he took prescription meds and speed to get through.

He knelt and thought about his life. When he was high, his mind raced, and he felt invincible. He felt as if he had everything together. Like he was a train moving fast down a track that no one could stop. That train had been gaining speed in the last year, and when he didn't have his drugs, he often felt like he was coming off the tracks. It would all work for him if he could just keep things going. He had quit his job as a mason and cooked methamphetamine full time. He rationalized that he could make more money, plus he didn't have to spend money on his habit.

His PO friend Jo wouldn't approve, but she didn't really understand what it was like. No one did. It didn't help to have friends if it meant having to live without meth. Even meeting Katie hadn't made him want to quit. She'd have to accept him the way he was, and he'd help her out if she didn't ask him to change too much. They'd both had hard lives, so maybe she could understand what made him tick.

He would do what this crazy fucker wanted him to do, and then he'd be on his way. He knelt for what seemed like an hour but in reality was only a couple of minutes. Then Don said, "Good, now get up. We're going inside to pray."

Don directed Rick down into a stone structure built right into the ground. Once inside, he pulled a rug away from the floor, revealing a trapdoor. They descended into a subbasement dug into the earth. Don shone a flashlight ahead of them and directed Rick to "Kneel and pray here." Rick was surrounded by fieldstone and mortar in this tiny little basement.

"If I pray, then I get to go?"

"I'll help you go myself," Don said to him. "Shoot your sin again before God and seek forgiveness."

Rick had never injected himself this close together and didn't quite know what effect it would have, but he was willing to do what it took to keep his train on the track. He removed his kit, cutting the meth, and felt the gun to his head, "Do it now."

Again he hesitated, unsure about what using this much methamphetamine would do to him, but he shot up before kneeling on the cold earthen floor. He put his hands together in prayer and died quietly of an overdose. His hemorrhaging brain caused blood to drip dramatically out of both his eyes.

Don saw the blood, knew that it was a sign of God's will, gathered up the kit, placed it back inside Rick's pocket, and then tied his hands together. He rigged up a rope system that would hold Rick in a kneeling prayer position indefinitely. Before closing the basement door, Don took a last satisfied look at the sinner he had brought to salvation and then left him in this cold, dark, secret place.

Chapter 38

DON SMILED EVER SO SLIGHTLY as he came back to the present. "He was a sinner, and he's repenting, God have mercy on his soul." Don was almost singing in a monotone voice like the ones Jo remembered priests using during Catholic mass. "He will have mercy on your soul. Kneel and pray to God."

He pointed the gun at Jo, who didn't move. Somehow she knew she needed to keep him talking. "Why does God need to have mercy on my soul?" Her knees felt weak, and the room was closing in, but she struggled to stay focused. The stench of rotting flesh helped her to stay in touch with her anger. She thought about the young man she had thought of more as a son than a former client.

Don again resumed in his monotone voice, "You have sinned in the eyes of the Lord. You have committed adultery. God have mercy on your soul." Frank was leaning against the wall and hugging himself. He flinched as Don spoke up again.

"They must be preserved so that their prayers are pure. We will cleanse the sins of the world."

Jo felt a keen desire to see this man dead. After what he had done to Rick, he didn't deserve to go on breathing. She could easily pull out the gun and end his days right here.

This must be how murderers feel, she thought. *But what would Zoey think if I killed this sorry lunatic?*

Jo could almost hear Zoey's response in her head: *"You're coping with reality far better than he is. He's not responsible for his actions, but you are."*

Jo felt suddenly ill, but the thought of Zoey had given her an inspiration. She pushed on. "Thou shalt not kill. You are the sinner; now give me the gun."

Don seemed shocked at her reply.

She found it hard not to lunge at him and pound him into a pulp. She was getting fuel from the anger and disgust at what she was experiencing. He seemed to be spacing out, so she spoke up again.

"Don, listen to me. This is wrong. God doesn't want you to do this for Him. Sinners will face God in their own time. Killing is a sin." She hadn't thought about the wisdom of going at him with this tact, but she was in survival mode.

"You don't know how it is. I am the chosen one." Don pointed to his chest with his good hand. His face was red with anger.

"You aren't stupid, Don. I see how you put this whole cabin together. That took some smarts. Take time to think this through."

Pausing for a moment, Don suddenly said, "Upstairs, now!" Neither of his hostages hesitated. They bounded up and out of the cryptlike basement.

As soon as she made it into the primary structure, Jo bent over, holding her knees and gasping. While she had not been conscious of holding her breath, she realized that she had instinctively stopped breathing the foul air.

Jo needed a plan. A way out. The gravity of Don's plans felt like an ominous cloud. She desperately wanted out of the cabin and away from him, away from the smell and image of Rick, and away from Don's sick and twisted mind.

"Don, look at me! Who am I?"

"You are Eve, born of man."

"What is my name?"

He sat down on a chair and scratched his face. He was holding the gun with his injured arm, resting it in his lap.

Jo saw her chance and lunged for the gun while pushing the chair over backwards. As he toppled, Don squeezed off a round. Jo felt a burning hot sensation starting in her left forearm and searing into her upper arm.

The recoil from the gunfire sent Don hurling the rest of the way backward in his chair. As he hit the ground, another shot rang out, ricocheting off the stone walls of the bunker. Jo and Frank both hit the floor. The bullet bounced several times before ending in a metallic thud.

When Jo looked up, Don was standing over her. "You dumb bitch! Look at what you've done. You are not pure. You cannot atone purely!"

174

Chapter 39

REE AND ZOEY HAD BEEN SITTING in reflective silence for nearly half an hour. Zoey was thinking about getting up to walk off some of her stress when two shots rang out. Boom…Boom.

Her heart pounded in her chest, and adrenalin surged in her limbs. She sprang up.

"Let's get them. Jo's in trouble."

Ree grabbed Zoey's arm and held her back until she looked at her.

"Get who? Slow down. What are you planning?"

"Sandy and Tanner. We have to go in there."

Ree relaxed and let go of her once she was assured she was not going to bust down the bunker door. Sandy and Tanner ran up to them.

"We have to do something," Zoey pleaded. "I need to get in there and talk to him. I'm a trained psychologist. I can work with him."

Tanner and Sandy seemed to be processing this information for a second before Tanner spoke up. "I'm the only armed person here, so it's going to be me going in first. Ree, can you trail behind for support? Let's hope we don't need you for medical help, but bring your bag. Sandy and Zoey, we need you on the tunnel door. If I give two radio clicks, come in from the front. If I give one, come in from the tunnel. Zoey, if we need you, I'll make several clicks. Sandy, don't let her move in unplanned." He looked around and waited for arguments.

Hearing none, he repeated, "One click—tunnel, two clicks—front door, several clicks—bring the shrink in for a consult."

Tanner crept up to the door with his gun drawn and out in front of him. Ree followed close behind. As soon as they were at the main entrance, Zoey made her way to the tunnel entrance to assume her post.

After only two minutes, she heard several clicks. She ran toward the cabin's front door. "Hold up!" Sandy trotted alongside, and they entered the cabin together.

The first thing Zoey saw when they entered was a gun held to Jo's head. Tanner and Don were in a standoff, and Jo's arm was a bloody mess. For an instant, the absurd thought passed through her mind, *"And this woman expects me to move in with her?"* Her heart sank into her stomach, and she couldn't think. Sandy placed a hand on Zoey's arm, whispering, "She needs you. You can do this."

Tanner broke the silence, "Frank, get out of here."

"No! He must repent. He must pay for his sins. I will bring him to repent."

In spite of her dire circumstances, Jo spoke up, "Rick is repenting right now down in the basement of this place. He's dead. Don brought him here to repent."

Zoey bolstered her resolve to talk him out of this. "Don, I'm Zoey, and I'm a psychologist. I can help you."

"No, you can't. You tie me up and shove pills down my throat. Pills that make me feel dead inside."

"I can give you some peace. You've been working very hard. You haven't slept for days. I can help you find some rest. Do you want to rest?"

Don appeared to be listening and then answered, "I must cleanse the world of sin. If I don't, the world will come to an end. Nuclear annihilation. The apocalypse. Our skin will melt from the impurity of so much sinning. Here, though, the end of the world can't get to me. The walls are too thick. I'm the chosen one. I must bring them to God."

"How many of them are there, Don?"

"I don't know…thousands, millions."

"How do you know you're the chosen one?" She was speaking in a gentle tone.

"Kill all of them. Bring them to God to repent."

"We're not sinners, Don. And you don't have to save the world. I can give you peace. You can rest then. It's time to rest. Inside, you're a good person. A loving and compassionate person, a kind person, a person of God." Zoey looked up to show him that they both had the same connection to God. "If you kill innocent people, that's wrong, isn't it?" He nodded yes.

The high-pitched sound of snowmobiles could be heard as they rushed toward the cabin. *Great timing*, Jo thought to herself. Don had a gun to her head, and Zoey was making some progress in de-escalating the situation and bringing him back to reality. Who knew what effect this would have on things?

Sandy backed out of the cabin, presumably to tell the snowmobilers to stand back and let things continue inside. Jo felt better about having more law enforcement and firepower on hand. Her arm ached so much she could feel each of her heartbeats as a pain-filled thud. The muscle had spasmed, and she couldn't move her hand at all. Bringing it up painfully, she tucked it into her collar for the support and the elevation.

Don was holding the gun with his wounded hand, and she worried about his ability to control his trigger finger. If he was in as much pain as she was, he had to be about to crack. On top of that, he had spent the last twelve-plus hours walking through the woods in blizzard conditions. She regretted her earlier attempt to overpower him, for obvious reasons.

"All people have sinned, Don. Even you. God is loving. God forgives." Zoey talked to him in low, comforting tones. "Tell me what you know about how God is loving."

Zoey had his full attention now. "Look, Karen, I know you want the best for me. I know you're right, I just can't go through all this again." *Karen?* Don must have been seeing a therapist at some point.

Off to her right, Jo noticed an officer entering the bunker. Maybe Sandy couldn't get him to back off. Then she heard the distinct sound of a rifle click. She didn't dare move while Don held the gun aimed at her head, but she assumed that the cavalry had arrived.

Zoey must have heard the sound, too.

Jo was stunned to see Zoey take a deliberate step forward, placing herself between the doorway and Don, shielding both Jo and Don from a sniper shot.

Jo had the sinking feeling that this standoff was going to end badly. She couldn't understand what Zoey was doing. Why had she come down into this hellhole, anyway? Why couldn't she have stayed outside until it was all over. Didn't she know that she was scaring Jo to death? Nothing Don had done so far had injected such terror in her as the step Zoey had just taken.

"Tell me what you're hearing, Don. Who is talking to you?"

Don didn't respond but seemed to be struggling with his own internal thought process. "God is loving. God is not hateful."

"Listen to me, Don. It's time to rest; time to be a good, loving person. Show us that you are, and let her go. I promise you will be able to rest. I can help you. I can help you with Jean. I promise to help you."

Don was loosening his grip on Jo and relaxing. He was giving in. He took the gun from Jo's head, and she walked out of his one-armed hold. She turned around so that her back wouldn't be toward him.

"That's right, Don. Everything will be all right now," Zoey said.

Then he turned the gun and placed it against his own head.

"No, Don. That's not the answer. I can help you rest. I can." Zoey's voice had lost its gentle tone.

BOOM! A thunderous explosion rocked the bunker.

Jo found herself watching the back of Don's head burst apart, sending brain and blood splatter everywhere as he fell to the floor. She ran to Zoey and turned her away from the sight. They held onto each other. Ree pulled them out of the cabin and into the daylight. Sandy ran to Ree, and they all stood there watching the personnel who had been waiting outside rush into the dark hole that contained so much horror.

After a moment of shocked silence, Ree took charge of Jo's injured arm, yelling out, "Hey! She needs a ride to the hospital. We need a driver!"

Chapter 40

THE RIDE IN WAS PAINFULLY BUMPY. Jo was able to focus enough to thank Zoey for her intervention with Don. She could tell Zoey was having a tough time, struggling with her conflicting feelings. On the one hand, Jo was alive. On the other, a severely mentally ill man was dead, and she had failed to prevent him from committing suicide.

With her good hand, Jo reached out for Zoey. "It's not your fault, you know."

"I know, but I'm going to replay this a thousand times in my head. Could I have said something else? Something that would have helped him see that he could be helped?" A tortured look crossed Zoey's pale features. Then she seemed to get herself under control and said to Jo, "I'm so glad you made it out of there." She hugged Jo fiercely.

Ree joined them for the sled ride to the Hammond and the ambulance ride to Duluth while Sandy retrieved their car and joined them at the hospital.

The doctors pulled a bullet from Jo's left bicep that had lodged in the bone. The bicep had to be reattached with screws following the removal. When she started to wake up, Jo was experiencing major pain even through serious painkillers. She could hear her friends playing poker on her bedside table. Zoey, Ree, Sandy, and Jo's good friends from the Valley—Kathy and Donna—were trying to subdue their usual hooting and hollering following each win.

When she came to enough, she stammered, "My deal; seven card no peek; aces, deuces, and one-eyed jacks wild." She could tell she was slurring her words, as it seemed to take an eternity to speak that one sentence. Zoey came rushing over and placed her hand on Jo's good arm, and her cheek against Jo's. "It's so good to see you awake."

"What does a girl have to do to get a decent cup of coffee around here?" Jo slurred out.

Zoey waved her hand at the group. "Can someone get my beautiful but seriously addicted girlfriend a cup of coffee?" Ree hopped up and left in search of a gourmet stand. Everyone else gathered around to behold the spectacle of her awakening.

"Some vacation," she teased.

"Trouble does have a way of finding you," offered her best friend and neighbor, Kathy. "Your dad has been calling. As soon as you're up to it, you better call him back. We told him you're fine, but he won't give up until he hears from you personally."

"Great. I hope he didn't flip out on you."

"Let's say he's really concerned."

"He must be insane with worry." She paused a little after the word *insane*. "He'll yell at me, tell me he loves me, and then try to get me to come to Florida to visit him." Jo was speaking a little more coherently now.

They all laughed at the same time.

"What? That is exactly what he said to you, isn't it?"

Kathy nodded and imitated him, "Well, tell her to stop chasing after those monsters. Good god. Let the police do that. What is she thinking? Well, tell her I love her, and that she's always welcome here. She can bring her friends, too."

Jo looked up at Zoey. "How are you?" She remembered Zoey's guilt over not being able to stop Don from killing himself.

"Better now. You know they said you would be fine, but until you came to, I couldn't help but worry. How much pain are you in?" Zoey gently pulled a lock of hair out of Jo's face.

"It hurts like crazy, but I think these drugs are pretty good." She looked down at her arm to see a large soft cast. Her hand was so swollen that the skin on her fingers looked tight. "I guess I won't be dealing anytime soon." She wiggled her fingers a tiny bit.

"We've been playing a hand for you. You're down two bucks," Sandy piped up.

"Oh thanks, guys, so if you hadn't played for me, I'd be even?"

Kathy edged her way into Jo's vision, "Hey, buddy."

"Hey. Good to see you. Is Donna here, too?"

"Over here."

"Hey. Thanks for coming. You're the best." Jo was clearly still a little loopy. Ree walked back in with gourmet coffees for everyone. Ree knew that the massive dose of anesthetic Jo had received for surgery would wreak havoc with her digestive system, so she'd brought her a latte and instructed her to take it easy.

"So, Doc, how am I?" Jo inquired.

"Well, given that the bullet was lodged in your bone, you're going to have a lot of pain. They successfully reattached your bicepial tendon and were able to clean up some of the other wreckage caused by the bullet. You'll need some serious pain meds for a while. You'll have to do physical therapy to regain your mobility, but then you should be fine."

"One hundred percent?" Jo asked hopefully.

"If you behave yourself," replied Ree.

"How long will I be out of commission?"

"You won't be able to work or do much of anything for three weeks, then you can start PT. After you give PT an honest effort, I'd say you could be fully functional in a couple of months."

Jo nodded. "When can I get out of here?"

"Another day or two, depending."

"We'll stick around until you get out," Sandy said.

"Really, it's OK. You don't have to. We'll be back finishing up our vacation in a couple of days." That made the group laugh again.

"Let's see how you feel about that once your anesthesia fully wears off," Ree said, as she looked at Jo's heart and oxygen monitors.

"Wow, look at that view." Jo looked out at Lake Superior and the historic lift bridge.

"I pulled some strings," Ree said with a smile.

"How's Bruns?" Jo asked.

"He's hanging in. It was touch and go. Had to have surgery and a transfusion. One of his lungs collapsed. If he makes it out of recovery with no major infections, he should be fine."

Nate stuck his funny-looking head around the door jam. The sight of him did Jo's heart good. She loved how his small head didn't quite fit his big body.

"Hey," he said. "What did I tell you? You weren't supposed to hang out with paranoid psychos on your vacation."

"I couldn't help it, Nate. They find me, I swear!"

"Well, I'm glad you're going to be OK." Nate cleared his throat. "I guess it might be a little late now, but those serial numbers did come back as stolen merchandise. I guess Rick was fencing the stuff."

"Nate, your genius astounds me sometimes," Jo said. The mention of Rick's name hurt somewhere deeper than all of the physical pain she was feeling.

"Umm, are you up for more visitors? There's someone here who'd like to meet you. She says Rick never stopped talking about you, so she wanted to see you for herself."

"Katie?"

"Yep. She's got something on her mind." Nate motioned for the group of friends to clear the room and give Jo some space.

Katie had on jeans, a sweatshirt, and too much makeup. As soon as she plopped in her chair, she crossed her arms.

"So, you're Jo."

"Almost, I'm still pretty drowsy."

"Rick thought you walked on water. He wouldn't want you to feel bad about...you know...how things ended up."

"What really happened, Katie? Were you there?"

"Well, I didn't stay in the car when he went into the woods that last time. I wanted to hang out with him, you know? He was always so nice to me, and after the family I came from...anyway, he was good to me," she sniffed a little.

"He wouldn't let me get started on meth. I didn't really want to, either. I'd seen what it did to my brothers and their customers. Umm," she seemed suddenly aware that there was a police detective standing at the door.

"Anyway, we drank together and talked about getting a regular business going, like maybe an art store or something. People are so crazy about art around here," Katie trailed off and seemed to be temporarily at a loss for words.

Jo was feeling sleepy again, but she tried to stay present. She sensed that this was a conversation that couldn't wait.

"Katie, you can still do that, you know. You can be an artist or own an art store. You've got your whole life to do what you want to do. Start where you are, and go for it."

"Ha! He always said you were like this, and I never believed him." The teenager looked wistful, "You might not be so hopeful about me if you knew what I did."

"OK, go ahead and give me the test."

"I left him there. He said he was going to shoot something for dinner. We were all out of cash, because of the wrecked loot…." Again, she glanced in Nate's direction before continuing, "So, like, that was his solution. I hate seeing things die." Katie choked up for about thirty seconds, and Jo was worried she was going to pass out before the important part of the story.

"So, I went back to the car to wait until he was done hunting, and I took some pills. Not meth… some pain meds to take the edge off. When I heard the shot, I figured, OK, he's done with that mess, and I headed back toward the shack.

"I knew something hinky was going on when I saw this big ugly guy skulking around in the woods near Rick's clearing. I stayed away and hid behind some trees, 'cuz I've learned to keep still and shut my mouth when shit happens. I really shoulda' screamed or somethin', though. He took Rick's gun, and before I knew it, he was marching Rick off with his hands up."

Katie broke off, looked up at the ceiling as if she couldn't go on.

"It's OK," Jo said with a tenderness as deep as the girl's distress. "Then what happened?"

"That's all I know. I went back to the car and waited a really long time. All that while, I was as scared as I could be that that ugly bastard would come back for me. I waited a really long time, over an hour. But I knew if I stayed there, I would be next. I just knew it."

"You're probably right. Look what happened to me," Jo pointed to her arm and tried to get the girl to smile, even though the thought of Rick's final hours was almost more than she could bear herself.

"But I left him there, with that crazy guy."

"You're just a kid, Katie," and Jo knew kids better than anyone. She had coaxed, cajoled, threatened, and even locked them up when she needed to. She used whatever was necessary to get them to turn their lives around.

"There wasn't anything you could do to change what happened. I'm glad Rick had you for a friend, though. He probably liked you as much as you liked him. His time was up, I guess, plus it didn't help that he was on meth. It probably made him a lot more vulnerable in the situation." She let that sink in.

"I can see you're a survivor, though, and you've still got a long time to get it right. Promise me you'll try."

The girl nodded through her tears.

Chapter 41

Jo was true to her word, and she and Zoey finished their vacation out at Sandy and Ree's guest cabin in Big Noise. Jo lounged around the cabin while Zoey tended to her, read novels, and fine-tuned her next semester's lessons. On the last evening of the vacation, they celebrated with a poker party that included Kathy and Donna coming up for the night.

Donna, Zoey's good friend and co-researcher, asked her about how she was dealing with Don's suicide.

Zoey answered her honestly, "I'm struggling with it. I keep replaying it in my head." She tapped an index finger up against her temple.

"You did the best you could. You saved Jo."

"Intellectually, I know all this. I mean, when people want to kill themselves, realistically there isn't much you can do to stop them. This was just so intimate, you know. It's definitely impacting me."

Jo reached over with her good hand and took Zoey's hand.

"What further complicates this is that I have conflicting feelings about it. This guy killed a man Jo was close to. In a vile and disgusting way. Then I tried to talk him out of hurting himself. How can I be sure I was sincere in my effort?" she shook her head.

"I have an idea about how I might be able to get some closure, though. I know myself. If I don't do something, I'll keep thinking about this."

"What is it you need to do?" Jo was still holding onto Zoey's hand.

She looked around at the group, and everyone there was listening carefully. Zoey felt the warmth of their friendship as they all waited for her reply.

"I need to go back there. Back to the scene of the shooting. Do you

185

know someone with a snowmobile? Someone who can take me in there?" She looked around the group hopefully.

Ree spoke up, "You remember Sherry? The poet? We jumped her car." Zoey and Jo nodded.

"She actually has a couple of them. You never know how well they might be running, but we can definitely check. I bet I can round up a few for us to use. Let's do it tomorrow. I'll start making calls."

She looked around to see who was interested.

"We're in," Donna spoke for both herself and Kathy.

"Definitely," Sandy chimed in.

Chapter 42

THEY PULLED UP TO THE BUNKER at 10:15 the following morning on three borrowed snowmobiles and one sled. Zoey had called Jean to see if she was also interested in looking for closure by going to the scene. Jean met them at G's, and they all followed the trail into the bunker. They had to go especially slow, as Jo's arm was still quite painful. The crime scene unit as well as a coroner and several other official teams had made their way into the land where the bunker was located by snowmobile, so the track was easy to follow.

They pulled up and turned off the machines. Zoey and Jean stood silently staring at the structure before beginning to walk toward it. Jo had begun to walk with Zoey, but Zoey turned to her and said, "Please… can I do this alone first?"

Jo nodded and touched Zoey's face. "I'll be right out here."

Jean had already walked into the bunker, and Zoey waited a couple of more minutes before walking in herself. She was struck by how peaceful the structure seemed. The last thing she had seen here was Don's head exploding from the gunshot. The sound of the shot rang over and over in her head, concluding each round of their final conversation.

She walked into and out of each room, repeating the same ritual of standing and taking in the smells and details. She then walked down into the basement room. It took a moment for her eyes to adjust to the dimmer light. The crime scene technicians had cleaned up any sign of remains, but the smell of decomposition lingered in the small space.

She did a silent prayer for the life lost in this tiny space before walking back up into the main cabin structure. She found Jean sitting at the kitchen table. Zoey walked over to where Don had taken his life. She replayed their conversation one more time in her head. Just before he pulled the trigger, she remembered a peaceful expression washing over him. She closed her eyes and willed herself to make that her last memory of the event.

When she opened her eyes, Jean was taking out a piece of paper and flattening it onto the table. "I wrote something." She nodded toward the piece of paper. "I'd like to read it."

"Do you want the others?" Zoey asked.

"Yeah. OK. That would be all right."

Zoey walked up the stairs and motioned for the group to join them before descending back into the bunker. Once everyone had found a place to stand, Jean began reading.

Sleep, My Lost Love

I wrap you in a quilt called
forgiveness
Sewn from fragments of our early life,
cut, patched, and made whole again.

Tender moments under cover
The sharing of pain buried deep
We thought the demons were safely shrouded—
A father's son had been released.

I wrap you in a quilt called love
that now lies chastened and quiet
restful and redeemed
for the long night.

Chapter 43

JO AND ZOEY SPENT THE FINAL WEEKEND before Zoey was scheduled to return to work at Jo's house. Jo wouldn't make her scheduled return until later, after being liberated from the soft cast that went from her shoulder to her wrist. She would need to spend another week lying low before beginning physical therapy.

Sunday evening, they sat on the floor in front of the fireplace drinking decaffeinated coffee and munching from a bowl of popcorn.

Jo turned to Zoey. She hesitated before speaking.

"Maybe you can help me with something. I'm still struggling with what happened out there. It's all jumbled up in my head. But mostly I'm angry with Don. I'm so angry I can't see straight. I can't properly grieve for Rick because of my anger."

"Tell me what goes through your mind. What are your most persistent thoughts?"

"I'm so angry with him for killing Rick. I know Don's already dead, but if I could, I'd like to kill him myself. I'm even angry with you for trying to help him."

"You're angry with me?"

"Not all the time. I mean, of course you had to try to help him. He was sick."

Zoey hesitated and chose her words carefully. "Sometimes the things we react strongest to are things we don't like in ourselves."

"You think I'm like Don?" Jo didn't hide her shock. She looked like she was ready to jump up and bolt from the room.

"No, it's what you think that could be key here. Do you see yourself as someone who is chosen to save the world?"

Jo didn't hesitate when she answered, "Sometimes. But so do you. I think we're both like Don in that way."

"What?" Zoey could feel herself getting defensive.

"We both have savior complexes. We shouldn't have risked our lives for either Rick or Don. I took chances, but you did, too. And you do, every time you deal with a violent, mentally ill person. Even after Don shot me, you wanted to save him."

"I'm a psychologist. It's what I do."

"Yes, and I'm someone who helps kids. They're not just hoodlums or criminals to me. They need me, and sometimes, trouble happens. You're a psychologist. But you're a human being, too. And you could be hurt by one of your psychotic clients or students as easily as I could be hurt on the streets. You take chances for others. We just handle it differently."

"Way differently," Zoey said.

Jo kept trying, "I have always known I'm driven to help others. I think you are, too. I've never loved anyone the way I love you. I understood what you were saying when you said you didn't know if you could take worrying about me because of my job. It's not my job. It's me. And it's you. I felt that out there. It pissed me off that you had to help him. I wanted to kill him. It pissed me off more that you risked your life to try to save him."

Jo slouched, as if from the weight of this knowledge. "How do we live with knowing that we would both risk everything to help people?"

Zoey was impressed. Jo had worked it all out right in front of her. She felt herself relax. Jo was right. There was no way they could always protect each other from the trait that they both shared.

"Maybe that's why we fell in love?"

"Being in love is a risk. Living is a risk. We have to learn to deal with our compulsion to help, too." Jo seemed to be gaining a sense of clarity.

"We could try to limit it to things we can actually impact. And if there's something we can't do alone, maybe we can do it together."

"Who's crazier? Don or us?"

"Are you asking the psychologist, or the human?"

"I'm not really asking."

Zoey looked into Jo's eyes and saw herself. She knew that Jo was doing the same thing.

"We are in this together, aren't we?" Jo asked, her anger having completely vanished.

"I think it might have been easier thinking it was all you," Zoey said tentatively.

"Well, it's a position we can always fall back on."

About the Author

JEN WRIGHT lives with her partner and two dogs in Clover Valley, Minnesota, bordering Lake Superior's north shore. Many of her stories arise from her real-life professional experiences working in a corrections agency and supervising Juvenile Probation and Drug Court. She and her staff help young people and adults to reclaim their lives. Unlike Jo, her protagonist in *Killer Storm* and *Big Noise,* Jen only drinks decaffeinated coffee.

Clover Valley Press, LLC, specializes in producing quality books written by women of the northland.

For author guidelines or to purchase copies of our books, go to www.clovervalleypress.com.

CLOVER
VALLEY
PRESS

CPSIA information can be obtained at www.ICGtesting.com
Printed in the USA
LVOW13s2256050814

397658LV00026B/447/P